W9-AHG-698

Collins Readers

WarHorse

michael morpurgo

Published by Collins Education
An imprint of HarperCollins Publishers
77-85 Fulham Palace Road, London W6 8JB

Browse the complete Collins Education catalogue at
www.collinseducation.com

First published in Great Britain in 1982 by Kaye & Ward Ltd
Reissued in 2007 by Egmont UK Limited
This edition first published by HarperCollins Publishers in 2011

Text copyright © Michael Morpurgo 1982

Michael Morpurgo asserts the moral right to be identified as the
author of this work.

ISBN 978 0 00 743726 9

10 9 8 7 6 5 4 3 2

All rights reserved. No part of this publication may be reproduced,
stored in a retrieval system, or transmitted in any form or by any
means, electronic, mechanical, photocopying, recording or
otherwise, without the prior written permission of the Publisher or
a licence permitting restricted copying in the United Kingdom
issued by the Copyright Licensing Agency Ltd, 90 Tottenham Court
Road, London W1T 4LP.

British Library Cataloguing in Publication Data
A catalogue record of this book is available from the British Library

Cover copyright © 2006 from the poster for the National Theatre's
stage adaptation of War Horse, playing from October 2007
www.nationaltheatre.org.uk

Cover design for this edition by Paul Manning

MICHAEL MORPURGO

War Horse

Collins Readers

For Lettice

AUTHOR'S NOTE

Many people have helped me in the writing of this book.
In particular I want to thank Clare and Rosalind, Sebastian
and Horatio, Jim Hindson (veterinary surgeon), Albert
Weeks, the late Wilfred Ellis and the late Captain Budgett –
all three octogenarians in the parish of Iddesleigh.

AUTHOR'S NOTE

IN THE OLD SCHOOL THEY USE NOW FOR THE Village Hall, below the clock that has stood always at one minute past ten, hangs a small dusty painting of a horse. He stands, a splendid red bay with a remarkable white cross emblazoned on his forehead and with four perfectly matched white socks. He looks wistfully out of the picture, his ears pricked forward, his head turned as if he has just noticed us standing there.

To many who glance up at it casually, as they might do when the hall is opened up for Parish meetings, for harvest suppers or evening socials, it is merely a tarnished old oil painting of some unknown horse by a competent but anonymous artist. To them the picture is so familiar that it commands little attention. But those who look more closely will see, written in fading black copperplate writing across the bottom of the bronze frame:

Joey.
Painted by Captain James Nicholls, autumn 1914.

Some in the village, only a very few now and fewer as each year goes by, remember Joey as he was. His story is written so that neither he nor those who knew him, nor the war they lived and died in, will be forgotten.

CHAPTER 1

MY EARLIEST MEMORIES ARE A CONFUSION OF hilly fields and dark, damp stables, and rats that scampered along the beams above my head. But I remember well enough the day of the horse sale. The terror of it stayed with me all my life.

I was not yet six months old, a gangling, leggy colt who had never been further than a few feet from his mother. We were parted that day in the terrible hubbub of the auction ring and I was never to see her again. She was a fine working farm horse, getting on in years but with all the strength and stamina of an Irish draught horse quite evident in her fore and hind quarters. She was sold within minutes, and before I could follow her through the gates, she was whisked out of the ring and away. But somehow I was more difficult to dispose of. Perhaps it was the wild look in my eye as I circled the ring in a desperate search for my mother, or perhaps it was that none of the farmers and gypsies there were looking for a spindly-looking half-thoroughbred colt. But whatever the reason they were a long time haggling over how little I was worth before I heard the hammer go down and I was driven out through the gates and into a pen outside.

'Not bad for three guineas, is he? Are you, my little firebrand? Not bad at all.' The voice was harsh and thick with drink, and it belonged quite evidently to my owner. I shall not call him my master, for only one man was ever my master. My owner had a rope in his hand and was clambering into the pen followed by three or four of his red-faced friends. Each one carried a rope. They had taken off their hats and jackets and rolled up their sleeves; and they were all laughing as they came towards me. I had as yet been touched by no man and backed away from them until I felt the bars of the pen behind me and could go no further. They seemed to lunge at me all at once, but they were slow and I managed to slip past them and into the middle of the pen where I turned to face them again. They had stopped laughing now. I screamed for my mother and heard her reply echoing in the far distance. It was towards that cry that I bolted, half charging, half jumping the rails so that I caught my off foreleg as I tried to clamber over and was stranded there. I was grabbed roughly by the mane and tail and felt a rope tighten around my neck before I was thrown to the ground and held there with a man sitting it seemed on every part of me. I struggled until I was weak, kicking out violently every time I felt them relax, but they were too many and too strong for me. I felt the halter slip over my head and tighten around my neck and face. 'So you're quite a fighter, are you?' said my owner, tightening the rope and smiling through gritted teeth. 'I like a fighter. But I'll break you one way or the other. Quite the little fighting cock you are, but you'll be eating out of my hand quick as a twick.'

I was dragged along the lanes tied on a short rope to the tailboard of a farm cart so that every twist and turn wrenched at my neck. By the time we reached the farm lane and rumbled over the bridge into the stable yard that was to become my home, I was soaked with exhaustion and the halter had rubbed my face raw. My one consolation as I was hauled into the stables that first evening was the knowledge that I was not alone. The old horse that had been pulling the cart all the way back from market was led into the stable next to mine. As she went in she stopped to look over my door and nickered gently. I was about to venture away from the back of my stable when my new owner brought his crop down on her side with such a vicious blow that I recoiled once again and huddled into the corner against the wall. 'Get in there you old ratbag,' he bellowed. 'Proper nuisance you are Zoey, and I don't want you teaching this young 'un your old tricks.' But in that short moment I had caught a glimpse of kindness and sympathy from that old mare that cooled my panic and soothed my spirit.

I was left there with no water and no food while he stumbled off across the cobbles and up into the farmhouse beyond. There was the sound of slamming doors and raised voices before I heard footsteps running back across the yard and excited voices coming closer. Two heads appeared at my door. One was that of a young boy who looked at me for a long time, considering me carefully before his face broke into a beaming smile. 'Mother,' he said deliberately. 'That will be a wonderful and brave horse. Look how he holds his head.' And then, 'Look at him, Mother, he's wet through to the skin. I'll have to rub him down.'

'But your father said to leave him, Albert,' said the boy's mother. 'Said it'll do him good to be left alone. He told you not to touch him.'

'Mother,' said Albert, slipping back the bolts on the stable door. 'When father's drunk he doesn't know what he's saying or what he's doing. He's always drunk on market days. You've told me often enough not to pay him any account when he's like that. You feed up old Zoey, Mother, while I see to him. Oh, isn't he grand, Mother? He's red almost, red-bay you'd call him, wouldn't you? And that cross down his nose is perfect. Have you ever seen a horse with a white cross like that? Have you ever seen such a thing? I shall ride this horse when he's ready. I shall ride him everywhere and there won't be a horse to touch him, not in the whole parish, not in the whole county.'

'You're barely past thirteen, Albert,' said his mother from the next stable. 'He's too young and you're too young, and anyway father says you're not to touch him, so don't come crying to me if he catches you in there.'

'But why the divil did he buy him, Mother?' Albert asked. 'It was a calf we wanted, wasn't it? That's what he went in to market for, wasn't it? A calf to suckle old Celandine?'

'I know dear, your father's not himself when he's like that,' his mother said softly. 'He says that Farmer Easton was bidding for the horse, and you know what he thinks of that man after that barney over the fencing. I should imagine he bought it just to deny him. Well that's what it looks like to me.'

'Well I'm glad he did, Mother,' said Albert, walking slowly towards me, pulling off his jacket. 'Drunk or not, it's the best thing he ever did.'

'Don't speak like that about your father, Albert. He's been through a lot. It's not right,' said his mother. But her words lacked conviction.

Albert was about the same height as me and talked so gently as he approached that I was immediately calmed and not a little intrigued, and so stood where I was against the wall. I jumped at first when he touched me but could see at once that he meant me no harm. He smoothed my back first and then my neck, talking all the while about what a fine time we would have together, how I would grow up to be the smartest horse in the whole wide world, and how we would go out hunting together. After a bit he began to rub me gently with his coat. He rubbed me until I was dry and then dabbed salted water onto my face where the skin had been rubbed raw. He brought in some sweet hay and a bucket of cool, deep water. I do not believe he stopped talking all the time. As he turned to go out of the stable I called out to him to thank him and he seemed to understand for he smiled broadly and stroked my nose. 'We'll get along, you and I,' he said kindly. 'I shall call you Joey, only because it rhymes with Zoey, and then maybe, yes maybe because it suits you. I'll be out again in the morning – and don't worry, I'll look after you. I promise you that. Sweet dreams, Joey.'

'You should never talk to horses, Albert,' said his mother from outside. 'They never understand you. They're stupid creatures. Obstinate and stupid, that's what your father says, and he's known horses all his life.'

'Father just doesn't understand them,' said Albert. 'I think he's frightened of them.'

I went over to the door and watched Albert and his mother walking away and up into the darkness. I knew then that I had found a friend for life, that there was an instinctive and immediate bond of trust and affection between us. Next to me old Zoey leant over her door to try to touch me, but our noses would not quite meet.

CHAPTER 2

THROUGH THE LONG HARD WINTERS AND HAZY summers that followed, Albert and I grew up together. A yearling colt and a young lad have more in common than awkward gawkishness.

Whenever he was not at school in the village, or out at work with his father on the farm, he would lead me out over the fields and down to the flat, thistly marsh by the Torridge river. Here on the only level ground on the farm he began my training, just walking and trotting me up and down, and later on lunging me first one way and then the other. On the way back to the farm he would allow me to follow on at my own speed, and I learnt to come at his whistle, not out of obedience but because I always wanted to be with him. His whistle imitated the stuttering call of an owl – it was a call I never refused and I would never forget.

Old Zoey, my only other companion, was often away all day ploughing and harrowing, cutting and turning out on the farm and so I was left on my own much of the time. Out in the fields in the summer time this was bearable because I could always hear her working and call out to her from time to time, but shut in the loneliness of the stable in the winter, all day could pass without seeing or hearing a soul, unless Albert came for me.

As Albert had promised, it was he who cared for me, and protected me all he could from his father; and his father did not turn out to be the monster I had expected. Most of the time he ignored me and if he did look me over, it was always from a distance. From time to time he could even be quite friendly, but I was never quite able to trust him, not after our first encounter. I would never let him come too close, and would always back off and shy away to the other end of the field and put old Zoey between us. On every Tuesday however, Albert's father could still be relied upon to get drunk, and on his return Albert would often find some pretext to be with me to ensure that he never came near me.

On one such autumn evening about two years after I came to the farm Albert was up in the village church ringing the bells. As a precaution he had put me in the stable with old Zoey as he always did on Tuesday evenings. 'You'll be safer together. Father won't come in and bother you, not if you're together,' he'd say, and then he'd lean over the stable door and lecture us about the intricacies of bell-ringing and how he had been given the big tenor bell because they thought he was man enough already to handle it and that in no time he'd be the biggest lad in the village. My Albert was proud of his bell-ringing prowess and as Zoey and I stood head to tail in the darkening stable, lulled by the six bells ringing out over the dusky fields from the church, we knew he had every right to be proud. It is the noblest of music for everyone can share it – they have only to listen.

I must have been standing asleep for I do not recall hearing him approach, but quite suddenly there was the dancing light of a lantern at the stable door and the bolts were pulled back. I thought at first it might be Albert, but the bells were still ringing, and then I heard the voice that was unmistakably that of Albert's father on a Tuesday night after market. He hung the lantern up above the door and came towards me. There was a whippy stick in his hand and he was staggering around the stable towards me.

'So, my proud little devil,' he said, the threat in his voice quite undisguised. 'I've a bet on that I can't have you pulling a plough inside a week. Farmer Easton and the others at The George think I can't handle you. But I'll show 'em. You've been molly-coddled enough, and the time has come for you to earn your keep. I'm going to try some collars on you this evening, find one that fits, and then tomorrow we'll start ploughing. Now we can do it the nice way or the nasty way. Give me trouble and I'll whip you till you bleed.'

Old Zoey knew his mood well enough and whinnied her warning, backing off into the dark recesses of the stable, but she need not have warned me for I sensed his intention. One look at the raised stick sent my heart thumping wildly with fear. Terrified, I knew I could not run, for there was nowhere to go, so I put my back to him and lashed out behind me. I felt my hooves strike home. I heard a cry of pain and turned to see him crawling out of the stable door dragging one leg stiffly behind him and muttering words of cruel vengeance.

That next morning both Albert and his father came out together to the stables. His father was walking with a pronounced limp. They were carrying a collar each and I could see that Albert had been crying for his pale cheeks were stained with tears. They stood together at the stable door. I noticed with infinite pride and pleasure that my Albert was already taller than his father whose face was drawn and lined with pain. 'If your mother hadn't begged me last night, Albert, I'd have shot that horse on the spot. He could've killed me. Now I'm warning you, if that animal is not ploughing straight as an arrow inside a week, he'll be sold on, and that's a promise. It's up to you. You say you can deal with him, and I'll give you just one chance. He won't let me go near him. He's wild and vicious, and unless you make it your business to tame him and train him inside that week, he's going. Do you understand? That horse has to earn his keep like everyone else around here – I don't care how showy he is – that horse has got to learn how to work. And I'll promise you another thing, Albert, if I have to lose that bet, then he has to go.' He dropped the collar on the ground and turned on his heel to go.

'Father,' said Albert with resolution in his voice. 'I'll

train Joey – I'll train him to plough all right – but you must promise never to raise a stick to him again. He can't be handled that way, I know him, Father. I know him as if he were my own brother.'

'You train him, Albert, you handle him. Don't care how you do it. I don't want to know,' said his father dismissively. 'I'll not go near the brute again. I'd shoot him first.'

But when Albert came into the stable it was not to smoothe me as he usually did, nor to talk to me gently. Instead he walked up to me and looked me hard in the eye. 'That was divilish stupid,' he said sternly. 'If you want to survive, Joey, you'll have to learn. You're never to kick out at anyone ever again. He means it, Joey. He'd have shot you just like that if it hadn't been for Mother. It was Mother who saved you. He wouldn't listen to me and he never will. So never again Joey. Never.' His voice changed now, and he spoke more like himself. 'We have one week Joey, only one week to get you ploughing. I know with all that thoroughbred in you you may think it beneath you, but that's what you're going to have to do. Old Zoey and me, we're going to train you; and it'll be divilish hard work – even harder for you 'cos you're not quite the right shape for it. There's not enough of you yet. You won't much like me by the end of it, Joey. But Father means what he says. He's a man of his word. Once he's made up his mind, then that's that. He'd sell you on, even shoot you rather than lose that bet, and that's for sure.'

That same morning, with the mists still clinging to the fields and linked side by side to dear old Zoey in a collar that hung loose around my shoulders, I was led out on to Long Close and my training as a farmhorse began. As we took the strain together for the first time the collar rubbed at my skin and my feet sank deep into the soft ground with the effort of it. Behind, Albert was shouting almost continuously, flashing a whip at me whenever I hesitated or went off line, whenever he felt I was not giving it my best – and he knew. This was a different Albert. Gone were the gentle words and the kindnesses of the past. His voice had a harshness and a sharpness to it that would brook no refusal on my part. Beside me old Zoey leant into her collar and pulled silently, head down, digging in with her feet. For her sake and for my own sake, for Albert's too, I leant my weight into my collar and began to pull. I was to learn during that week the rudiments of ploughing like a farm horse. Every muscle I had ached with the strain of it; but after a night's good rest stretched out in the stable I was fresh again and ready for work the next morning.

Each day as I progressed and we began to plough more as a team, Albert used the whip less and less and spoke more gently to me again, until finally at the end of the week I was sure I had all but regained his affection. Then one afternoon after we had finished the headland around Long Close, he unhitched the plough and put an arm around each of us. 'It's all right now, you've done it my beauties. You've done it,' he said. 'I didn't tell you, 'cos I didn't want to put you off, but Father and Farmer Easton have been watching us from the house this afternoon.' He scratched us behind the ears and smoothed our noses. 'Father's won his bet and he told me at breakfast that if we finished the field today he'd forget all about the incident, and that you could stay on, Joey. So you've done it my beauty and I'm so proud of you I could kiss you, you old silly, but I won't do that, not with them watching. He'll let you stay now, I'm sure he will. He's a man of his word is my father, you can be sure of that – long as he's sober.'

It was some months later, on the way back from cutting the hay in Great Meadow along the sunken leafy lane that led up into the farmyard that Albert first talked to us of the war. His whistling stopped in mid-tune. 'Mother says there's likely to be a war,' he said sadly. 'I don't know what it's about, something about some old Duke that's been shot at somewhere. Can't think why that should matter to anyone, but she says we'll be in it all the same. But it won't affect us, not down here. We'll go on just the same. At fifteen I'm too young to go anyway – well that's what she said. But I tell you Joey, if there is a war I'd want to go. I think I'd make a good soldier, don't you? Look fine in a uniform, wouldn't I? And I've always wanted to march to the beat of a band. Can you imagine that, Joey? Come to that, you'd make a good war horse yourself, wouldn't you, if you ride as well as you pull, and I know you will. We'd make quite a pair. God help the Germans if they ever have to fight the two of us.'

One hot summer evening, after a long and dusty day in the fields, I was deep into my mash and oats, with Albert still rubbing me down with straw and talking on about the abundance of good straw they'd have for the winter months, and about how good the wheat straw would be for the thatching they would be doing, when I heard his father's heavy steps coming across the yard towards us. He was calling out as he came. 'Mother,' he shouted. 'Mother, come out Mother.' It was his sane voice, his sober voice and was a voice that held no fear for me. 'It's war, Mother. I've just heard it in the village. Postman came in this afternoon with the news. The devils have marched into Belgium. It's certain for sure now. We declared war yesterday at eleven o'clock. We're at war with the Germans. We'll give them such a hiding as they won't ever raise their fists again to anyone. Be over in a few months. It's always been the same. Just because the British lion's sleeping they think he's dead. We'll teach them a thing or two, Mother – we'll teach them a lesson they'll never forget.'

Albert had stopped brushing me and dropped the straw on the ground. We moved over towards the stable door. His mother was standing on the steps by the door of the farmhouse. She had her hand to her mouth. 'Oh dear God,' she said softly. 'Oh dear God.'

CHAPTER 3

GRADUALLY DURING THAT LAST SUMMER ON THE farm, so gradually that I had hardly noticed it, Albert had begun riding me out over the farm to check the sheep. Old Zoey would follow along behind and I would stop every now and then to be sure she was still with us. I do not even remember the first time he put a saddle on me, but at some time he must have done so for by the time war was declared that summer Albert was riding me out to the sheep each morning and almost every evening after his work. I came to know every lane in the parish, every whispering oak tree and every banging gate. We would splash through the stream under Innocent's Copse and thunder up Ferny

Piece beyond. With Albert riding me there was no hanging on the reins, no jerking on the bit in my mouth, but always a gentle squeeze with the knees and a touch with his heels was enough to tell me what he wanted of me. I think he could have ridden me even without that so well did we come to understand each other. Whenever he was not talking to me, he would whistle or sing all the time, and that seemed somehow to reassure me.

The war hardly touched us on the farm to start with. With more straw still to turn and stack for the winter, old Zoey and I were led out every morning early into the fields to work. To our great relief, Albert had now taken over most of the horse work on the farm, leaving his father to see to the pigs and the bullocks, to check the sheep, and to mend fences and dig the ditches around the farm, so that we scarcely saw him for more than a few minutes each day. Yet in spite of the normality of the routine, there was a growing tension on the farm, and I began to feel an acute sense of foreboding. There would be long and heated exchanges in the yard, sometimes between Albert's father and mother, but more often, strangely enough, between Albert and his mother.

'You mustn't blame him, Albert,' she said one

morning, turning on him angrily outside the stable door. 'He did it all for you, you know. When Lord Denton offered to sell him the farm ten years ago he took out the mortgage so that you'd have a farm of your own when you grow up. And it's the mortgage that worries him sick and makes him drink. So if he isn't himself from time to time you've no call to keep on about him. He's not as well as he used to be and be can't put in the work on the farm like he used. He's over fifty, you know – children don't think of their fathers as being old or young. And it's the war too. The war worries him Albert. He's worried prices will be falling back, and I think in his heart of hearts he feels he should be soldiering in France – but he's too old for that. You've got to try to understand him, Albert. He deserves that much.'

'You don't drink, Mother,' Albert replied vehemently. 'And you've got worries just like he has, and anyway if you did drink you wouldn't get at me as he does. I do all the work I can, and more, and still he never stops complaining that this isn't done and that isn't done. He complains every time I take Joey out in the evening. He doesn't even want me to go off bell-ringing once a week. It's not reasonable, Mother.'

'I know that, Albert,' his mother said more gently now, taking his hand in both of hers. 'But you must try to see the good in him. He's a good man – he really is. You remember him that way too, don't you?'

'Yes Mother, I remember him like that,' Albert acknowledged, 'but if only he wouldn't keep on about Joey as he does. After all, Joey works for his living now and he has to have time off to enjoy himself, just as I do.'

'Of course dear,' she said, taking his elbow and walking him up towards the farmhouse, 'but you know how he feels about Joey, don't you? He bought him in a fit of pique and has regretted it ever since. As he says, we really only need one horse for the farmwork, and that horse of yours eats money. That's what worries him. Farmers and horses, it's always the same. My father was like it too. But he'll come round if you're kind with him – I know he will.'

But Albert and his father scarcely spoke to each other any more these days, and Albert's mother was used more and more by both as a go-between, as a negotiator. It was on a Wednesday morning with the war but a few weeks old, that Albert's mother was again arbitrating between them in the yard outside. As usual Albert's father had come home drunk from the market the night before. He said he had forgotten to take back the Saddleback boar they had borrowed to serve the sows and gilts. He had told Albert to do it, but Albert had objected strongly and an argument was brewing. Albert's father said that he 'had business to attend to' and Albert maintained he had the stables to clean out.

'Won't take you but half an hour, dear, to drive the boar back down the valley to Fursden,' Albert's mother said swiftly, trying to soften the inevitable.

'All right then,' Albert conceded, as he always did when his mother intervened, for he hated to upset her. 'I'll do it for you, Mother. But only on condition I can take Joey out this evening. I want to hunt him this winter and I have to get him fit.' Albert's father stayed silent and thin lipped, and I noticed then that he was looking straight at me. Albert turned, patted me gently on the nose, picked up a stick from the pile of lightings up against the woodshed, and made his way down towards the piggery. A few minutes later I saw him driving the great black and white boar out down the farm track towards the lane. I called out after him but he did not turn round.

Now if Albert's father came into the stable at all, it was always to lead out old Zoey. He left me alone these days. He would throw a saddle onto Zoey out in the yard and ride out onto the hills above the farmhouse to check the sheep. So it was nothing special when he came into the stable that morning and led Zoey out. But when he came back into the stable afterwards and began to sweet-talk me and held out a bucket of sweet-smelling oats, I was immediately suspicious. But the oats and my own inquisitiveness overcame my better judgement and he was able to slip a halter over my head before I could pull away. His voice however was unusually gentle and kind as he tightened the halter and reached out slowly to stroke my neck. 'You'll be all right, old son,' he said softly. 'You'll be all right. They'll look after you, promised they would. And I need the money, Joey, I need the money bad.'

CHAPTER 4

TYING A LONG ROPE TO THE HALTER HE WALKED me out of the stable. I went with him because Zoey was out there looking back over her shoulder at me and I was always happy to go anywhere and with anyone as long as she was with me. All the while I noticed that Albert's father was speaking in a hushed voice and looking around him like a thief.

He must have known that I would follow old Zoey, for he roped me up to her saddle and led us both quietly out of the yard down the track and over the bridge. Once in the lane he mounted Zoey swiftly and we trotted up the hill and into the village. He never spoke a word to either of us. I knew the road well enough of course for I had been there often enough with Albert, and indeed I loved going there because there were always other horses to meet and people to see. It was in the village only a short time before that I had met my first motor-car outside the Post Office and had stiffened with fear as it rattled past, but I had stood steady and I remember that Albert had made a great fuss of me after that. But now as we neared the village I could see that several motor-cars were parked up around the green and there was a greater gathering of men and horses than I had ever seen. Excited as I was, I remember that a sense of deep apprehension came over me as we trotted up into the village.

There were men in khaki uniforms everywhere; and then as Albert's father dismounted and led us up past the church towards the green a military band struck up a rousing, pounding march. The pulse of the great bass drum beat out through the village and there were children everywhere, some marching up and down with broomsticks over their shoulders and some leaning out of windows waving flags.

As we approached the flagpole in the centre of the green where the Union Jack hung limp in the sun against the white pole, an officer pushed through the crowd towards us. He was tall and elegant in his jodhpurs and Sam Brown belt, with a silver sword at his side. He shook Albert's father by the hand. 'I told you I'd come, Captain Nicholls, sir,' said Albert's father. 'It's because I need the money, you understand. Wouldn't part with a horse like this 'less I had to.'

'Well farmer,' said the officer, nodding his appreciation as he looked me over. 'I'd thought you'd be exaggerating when we talked in The George last evening. "Finest horse in the parish" you said, but then everyone says that. But this one is different – I can see that.' And he smoothed my neck gently and scratched me behind my ears. Both his hand and his voice were kind and I did not shrink away from him. 'You're right, farmer, he'd make a fine mount for any regiment and we'd be proud to have him – I wouldn't mind using him myself. No, I wouldn't mind at all. If he turns out to be all he looks, then he'd suit me well enough. Fine looking animal, no question about it.'

'Forty pounds you'll pay me, Captain Nicholls, like you promised yesterday?' Albert's father said in a voice that was unnaturally low, almost as if he did not want to be heard by anyone else. 'I can't let him go for a penny less. Man's got to live.'

'That's what I promised you last evening, farmer,' Captain Nicholls said, opening my mouth and examining my teeth. 'He's a fine young horse, strong neck, sloping shoulder, straight fetlocks. Done much work has he? Hunted him out yet, have you?'

'My son rides him out every day,' said Albert's father. 'Goes like a racer, jumps like a hunter he tells me.'

'Well,' said the officer, 'as long as our vet passes him as fit and sound in wind and limb, you'll have your forty pounds, as we agreed.'

'I can't be long, sir,' Albert's father said, glancing back over his shoulder. 'I have to get back. I have my work to see to.'

'Well, we're busy recruiting in the village as well as buying,' said the officer. 'But we'll be as quick as we can for you. True, there's a lot more good men volunteers than there are good horses in these parts, and the vet doesn't have to examine the men, does he? You wait here, I'll only be a few minutes.'

Captain Nicholls led me away through the archway opposite the public house and into a large garden beyond where there were men in white coats and a uniformed clerk sitting down at a table taking notes. I thought I heard old Zoey calling after me, so I shouted back to reassure her for I felt no fear at this moment. I was too interested in what was going on around me. The officer talked to me gently as we walked away, so I went along almost eagerly. The vet, a small, bustling man with a bushy black moustache, prodded me all over, lifted each of my feet to examine them – which I objected to – and then peered into my eyes and my mouth, sniffing at my breath. Then I was trotted round and round the garden before he pronounced me a perfect specimen. 'Sound as a bell. Fit for anything, cavalry or artillery,' were the words he used. 'No splints, no curbs, good feet and teeth. Buy him, Captain,' he said. 'He's a good one.'

I was led back to Albert's father who took the offered notes from Captain Nicholls, stuffing them quickly into his trouser pocket. 'You'll look after him, sir?' he said. 'You'll see he comes to no harm? My son's very fond of him you see.' He reached out and brushed my nose with his hand. There were tears filling his eyes. At that moment he became almost a likeable man for me. 'You'll be all right, old son,' he whispered to me. 'You won't understand and neither will Albert, but unless I sell you I can't keep up with the mortgage and we'll lose the farm. I've treated you bad – I've treated everyone bad. I know it and I'm sorry for it.' And he walked away from me leading Zoey behind him. His head was lowered and he looked suddenly a shrunken man.

It was then that I fully realised I was being abandoned and I began to neigh, a high-pitched cry of pain and anxiety that shrieked out through the village. Even old Zoey, obedient and placid as she always was, stopped and would not be moved on no matter how hard Albert's father pulled her. She turned, tossed up her head and shouted her farewell. But her cries became weaker and she was finally dragged away and out of my sight. Kind hands tried to contain me and to console me, but I was unconsolable.

I had just about given up all hope, when I saw my Albert running up towards me through the crowd, his face red with exertion. The band had stopped playing and the entire village looked on as he came up to me and put his arms around my neck.

'He's sold him, hasn't he?' he said quietly, looking up at Captain Nicholls who was holding me. 'Joey is my horse. He's my horse and he always will be, no matter who buys him. I can't stop my father from selling him, but if Joey goes with you, I go. I want to join up and stay with him.'

'You've the right spirit for a soldier, young man,' said the officer, taking off his peaked cap and wiping his brow with the back of his hand. He had black curly hair and a kind, open look on his face. 'You've the spirit but you haven't the years. You're too young and you know it. Seventeen's the youngest we take. Come back in a year or so and then we'll see.'

'I look seventeen,' Albert said, almost pleading. 'I'm bigger than most seventeen year olds.' But even as he spoke he could see he was getting nowhere. 'You won't take me then, sir? Not even as a stable boy? I'll do anything, anything.'

'What's your name, young man?' Captain Nicholls asked.

'Narracott, sir. Albert Narracott.'

'Well, Mr Narracott. I'm sorry I can't help you.' The officer shook his head and replaced his cap. 'I'm sorry, young man, regulations. But don't you worry about your Joey. I shall take good care of him until you're ready to join us. You've done a fine job on him. You should be proud of him – he's a fine, fine horse, but your father needed the money for the farm, and a farm won't run without money. You must know that. I like your spirit, so when you're old enough you must come and join the Yeomanry. We shall need men like you, and it will be a long war I fear, longer than people think. Mention my name. I'm Captain Nicholls, and I'd be proud to have you with us.'

'There's no way then?' Albert asked. 'There's nothing I can do?'

'Nothing,' said Captain Nicholls. 'Your horse belongs to the army now and you're too young to join up. Don't you worry – we'll look after him. I'll take personal care of him, and that's a promise.'

Albert wriggled my nose for me as he often did and stroked my ears. He was trying to smile but could not. 'I'll find you again, you old silly,' he said quietly. 'Wherever you are, I'll find you, Joey. Take good care of him, please sir, till I find him again. There's not another horse like him, not in the whole world – you'll find that out. Say you promise?'

'I promise,' said Captain Nicholls. 'I'll do everything I can.' And Albert turned and went away through the crowd until I could see him no more.

CHAPTER 5

IN THE FEW SHORT WEEKS BEFORE I WENT OFF TO war I was to be changed from a working farmhorse into a cavalry mount. It was no easy transformation, for I resented deeply the tight disciplines of the riding school and the hard hot hours out on manoeuvres on the Plain. Back at home with Albert I had revelled in the long rides along the lanes and over the fields, and the heat and the flies had not seemed to matter; I had loved the aching days of ploughing and harrowing alongside Zoey, but that was because there had been a bond between us of trust and devotion. Now there were endless tedious hours circling the school. Gone was the gentle snaffle bit that I was so used to, and in its place was an uncomfortable, cumbersome Weymouth that snagged the corners of my mouth and infuriated me beyond belief.

But it was my rider that I disliked more than anything in my new life. Corporal Samuel Perkins was a hard, gritty little man, an ex-jockey whose only pleasure in life seemed to be the power he could exert over a horse. He was universally feared by all troopers and horses alike. Even the officers, I felt, went in trepidation of him; for he knew it seemed all there was to know about horses and had the experience of a lifetime behind him. And he rode hard and heavy-handed. With him the whip and the spurs were not just for show.

He would never beat me or lose his temper with me, indeed sometimes when he was grooming me I think maybe he quite liked me and I certainly felt for him a degree of respect, but this was based on fear and not love. In my anger and unhappiness I tried several times to throw him off but never succeeded. His knees had a grip of iron and he seemed instinctively to know what I was about to do.

My only consolation in those early days of training were the visits of Captain Nicholls every evening to the stables. He alone seemed to have the time to come and talk to me as Albert had done before. Sitting on an upturned bucket in the corner of my stable, a sketch-book on his knees, he would draw me as he talked. 'I've done a few sketches of you now,' he said one evening, 'and when I've finished this one I'll be ready to paint a picture of you. It won't be Stubbs – it'll be better than Stubbs because Stubbs never had a horse as beautiful as you to paint. I can't take it with me to France – no point, is there? So I'm going to send it off to your friend Albert, just so that he'll know that I meant what I said when I promised I would look after you.' He kept looking up and down at me as he worked and I longed to tell him how much I wished he would take over my training himself and how hard the Corporal was and how my sides hurt and my feet hurt. 'To be honest with you, Joey, I hope this war will be over before he's old enough to join us because – you mark my words – it's going to be nasty, very nasty indeed. Back in the Mess they're all talking about how they'll set about Jerry, how the cavalry will smash through them and throw them clear back to Berlin before Christmas. It's just Jamie and me, we're the only ones that don't agree, Joey. We have our doubts, I can tell you that. We have our doubts. None of them in there seem to have heard of machine-guns and artillery. I tell you, Joey, one machine-gun operated right could wipe out an entire squadron of the best cavalry in the world – German or British. I mean, look what happened to the Light Brigade at Balaclava when they took on the Russian guns – none of them seem to remember that. And the French learnt the lesson in the Franco-Prussian War. But you can't say anything to them, Joey. If you do they call you defeatist, or some such rubbish. I honestly think that some of them in there only want to win this war if the cavalry can win it.'

He stood up, tucked his sketchbook under his arm and came over towards me and tickled me behind the ears. 'You like that old son, don't you? Below all that fire and brimstone you're a soppy old date at heart. Come to think of it we have a lot in common you and I. First, we don't much like it here and would rather be somewhere else. Second, we've neither of us ever been to war – never even heard a shot fired in anger, have we? I just hope I'm up to it when the time comes – that's what worries me more than anything, Joey. Because I tell you, and I haven't even told Jamie this –

I'm frightened as hell, so you'd better have enough courage for the two of us.'

A door banged across the yard and I heard the familiar sound of boots, crisp on the cobbles. It was Corporal Samuel Perkins passing along the lines of stables on his evening rounds, stopping at each one to check until at last he came to mine. 'Good evening, sir,' he said, saluting smartly. 'Sketching again?'

'Doing my best, Corporal,' said Captain Nicholls. 'Doing my best to do him justice. Is he not the finest mount in the entire squadron? I've never seen a horse so well put together as he is, have you?'

'Oh he's special enough to look at, sir,' said the Corporal of Horse. Even his voice put my ears back, there was a thin, acid tone to it that I dreaded. 'I grant you that, but looks aren't everything, are they, sir? There's always more to a horse than meets the eye, isn't that right, sir? How shall I put it, sir?'

'However you like, Corporal,' said Captain Nicholls somewhat frostily, 'but be careful what you say for that's my horse you're speaking about, so take care.'

'Let's say I feel he has a mind of his own. Yes, let's put it that way. He's good enough out on manoeuvres – a real stayer, one of the very best – but inside the school, sir, he's a devil, and a strong devil too. Never been properly schooled, sir, you can tell that. Farm-horse he is and farm trained. If he's to make a cavalry horse, sir, he'll have to learn to accept the disciplines. He has to learn to obey instantly and instinctively. You don't want a prima donna under you when the bullets start flying.'

'Fortunately, Corporal,' said Captain Nicholls. 'Fortunately this war will be fought out of doors and not indoors. I asked you to train Joey because I think you are the best man for the job – there's no one better in the squadron. But perhaps you should ease up on him just a bit. You've got to remember where he came from. He's a willing soul – he just needs a bit of gentle persuasion, that's all. But keep it gentle, Corporal, keep it gentle. I don't want him soured. This horse is going to carry me through the war and with any luck out the other side of it. He's special to me Corporal, you know that. So make sure you look after him as if he was your own, won't you? We leave for France in under a week now. If I had the time I'd be schooling him on myself, but I'm far too busy trying to turn troopers into mount-ed infantry. A horse may carry you through, Corporal, but he can't do your fighting for you. And there's some of them still think they'll only be needing their sabres when they get out there. Some of them really believe that flashing their sabres around will frighten Jerry all the way home. I tell you they have got to learn to shoot straight – we'll all have to learn to shoot straight if we want to win this war.'

'Yes sir,' said the corporal with a new respect in his voice. He was more meek and mild now than I had ever seen him.

'And Corporal,' said Captain Nicholls walking towards the stable door, 'I'd be obliged if you'd feed Joey up somewhat, he's lost a bit of condition, gone back a bit I'd say. I shall be taking him out myself on final manoeuvres in two or three days and I want him fit and shining. He's to look the best in the squadron.'

It was only in that last week of my military education that I began at last to settle into the work. Corporal Samuel Perkins seemed less harsh towards me after that evening. He used the spurs less and gave me more rein. We did less work now in the school and more formation work on the open plains outside the camp. I took the Weymouth bit more readily now and began to play with it between my teeth as I had always done with the snaffle. I began to appreciate the good food and the grooming and the buffing up, all the unending attention and care that was devoted to me. As the days passed I began to think less and less of the farm and old Zoey and of my early life. But Albert, his face and his voice stayed clear in my mind despite the unerring routine of the work that was turning me imperceptibly into an army horse.

By the time Captain Nicholls came to take me out on those last manoeuvres before we went to war I was already quite resigned to, even contented in my new life. Dressed now in field service marching order, Captain Nicholls weighed heavy on my back as the entire regiment moved out onto Salisbury Plain. I remember mostly the heat and the flies that day for there were hours of standing about in the sun waiting for things to happen. Then with the evening sun spreading and dying along the flat horizon the entire regiment lined up in echelon for the charge, the climax of our last manoeuvres.

The order was given to draw swords and we walked forward. As we waited for the bugle calls the air was electric with anticipation. It passed between every horse and his rider, between horse and horse, between trooper and trooper. I felt inside me a surge of such excitement that I found it difficult to contain myself. Captain Nicholls was leading his troop and alongside him rode his friend Captain Jamie Stewart on a horse I had never seen before. He was a tall, shining black stallion. As we walked forward I glanced up at him and caught his eye. He seemed to acknowledge it briefly. The walk moved into a trot and then into a canter. I heard the bugles blow and caught sight of his sabre pointing over my right ear. Captain Nicholls leant forward in the saddle and urged me into a gallop. The thunder and the dust and the roar of men's voices in my ears took a hold to me and held me at a pitch of exhilaration I had never before experienced. I flew over the ground way out ahead of the rest of them except for one. The only horse to stay with me was the shining black stallion. Although nothing was said between Captain Nicholls and Captain Stewart, I felt it was suddenly important that I should not allow this horse to get ahead of me. One look told me that he felt the same, for there was a grim determination in his eyes and his brow was furrowed with concentration. When we overran the 'enemy' position it was all our riders could do to bring us to a halt, and finally we stood nose to nose, blowing and panting with both captains breathless with exertion.

'You see, Jamie, I told you so,' said Captain Nicholls, and there was such pride in his voice as he spoke. 'This is the horse I was telling you about – found in deepest Devon – and if we had gone on much longer your Topthorn would have been struggling to stay with him. You can't deny it.'

Topthorn and I looked warily at each other at first. He was half a hand or more higher than me, a huge sleek horse that held his head with majestic dignity. He was the first horse I had ever come across that I felt could challenge me for strength, but there was also a kindness in his eye that held no threat for me.

'My Topthorn is the finest mount in this regiment, or any other,' said Captain Jamie Stewart. 'Joey might be faster, and all right I'll grant he looks as good as any horse I've ever seen pulling a milk float, but there's no one to match my Topthorn for stamina – why he could have gone on for ever and ever. He's an eight horse-power horse, and that's a fact.'

On the way back to the barracks that evening the two officers debated the virtues of their respective horses, whilst Topthorn and I plodded along shoulder to shoulder, heads hanging – our strength sapped by the sun and the long gallop. We were stabled side by side that night, and again on the boat the next day we found ourselves together in the bowels of the converted liner that was to carry us off to France and away to the war.

CHAPTER 6

THERE WAS ALL ABOUT US ON THE SHIP AN AIR of great exuberance and expectancy. The soldiers were buoyant with optimism, as if they were embarking on some great military picnic; it seemed none of them had a care in the world. As they tended us in our stalls the troopers joked and laughed together as I had never heard them before. And we were to need their confidence around us, for it was a stormy crossing and many of us became overwrought and apprehensive as the ship tossed wildly in the sea. Some of us kicked out at our stalls in a desperate effort to break free and to find ground that did not pitch and plunge under our feet, but the troopers were always there to hold us steady and to comfort us.

My comfort, however, came not from Corporal Samuel Perkins, who came to hold my head through the worst of it; for even when he patted me he did it in such a peremptory fashion that I did not feel he meant it. My comfort came from Topthorn who remained calm throughout. He would lean his great head over the stall and let me rest on his neck while I tried to obliterate from my mind the sinking surge of the ship and the noise of uncontrolled terror from the horses all around me.

But the moment we docked the mood changed. The horses recovered their composure with solid still land under their hooves once more, but the troopers fell silent and sombre as we walked past unending lines of wounded waiting to board the ship back to England. As we disembarked and were led away along the quayside Captain Nicholls walked by my head turning his eyes out to sea so that no one should notice the tears in them. The wounded were everywhere – on stretchers, on crutches, in open ambulances, and etched on every man was the look of wretched misery and pain. The tried to put a brave face on it, but even the jokes and quips they shouted out as we passed were heavy with gloom and sarcasm. No sergeant major, no enemy barrage could have silenced a body of soldiers as effectively as that terrible sight, for here for the first time the men saw for themselves the kind of war they were going into and there was not a single man in the squadron who seemed prepared for it.

Once out into the flat open country the squadron threw off its unfamiliar shroud of despondency and regained its jocular spirits. The men sang again in their saddles and laughed amongst themselves. It was to be a long, long march through the dust, all that day and the next. We would stop once every hour for a few minutes and would ride on until dusk before making camp near a village and always by a stream or a river. They cared for us well on that march, often dismounting and walking beside us to give us the rest we needed. But sweetest of all were the full buckets of cooling, quenching water they would bring us whenever we stopped beside a stream. Topthorn, I noticed, always shook his head in the water before he started to drink so that alongside him I was showered all over my face and neck with cooling water.

The mounts were tethered in horse lines out in the open as we had been on manoeuvres back in England.

So we were already hardened to living out. But it was colder now as the damp mists of autumn fell each evening and chilled us where we stood. We had plenty of fodder morning and evening, a generous ration of corn from our nosebags and we grazed whenever we could. Like the men we had to learn to live off the land as much as possible.

Every hour of the march brought us nearer the distant thunder of the guns, and at night now the horizon would be bright with orange flashes from one end to the other. I had heard the crack of rifle fire before back at the barracks and this had not upset me one bit, but the growling crescendo of the big guns sent tremors of fear along my back and broke my sleep into a succession of jagged nightmares. But whenever I woke, dragged back to consciousness by the guns, I found Topthorn was always by me and would breathe his courage into me to support me. It was a slow baptism of fire for me, but without Topthorn I think I should never have become accustomed to the guns, for the fury and the violence of the thunder as we came ever nearer to the front line seemed to sap my strength as well as my spirits.

On the march Topthorn and I walked always together, side by side, for Captain Nicholls and Captain Stewart were rarely apart. They seemed somehow separate in spirit from their heartier fellow officers. The more I got to know Captain Nicholls, the more I liked him. He rode me as Albert had, with a gentle hand and a firm grip of the knees, so that despite his size – and he was a big man – he was always light on me. And there was always some warm word of encouragement or gratitude after a long ride. This was a welcome contrast to Corporal Samuel Perkins who had ridden me so hard whilst in training. I caught sight of him from time to time and pitied the horse he rode.

Captain Nicholls did not sing or whistle as Albert had, but he talked to me from time to time when we were alone together. No one it appeared really knew where the enemy was. That he was advancing and that we were retreating was not in doubt. We were supposed to try to ensure that the enemy did not outflank us – we did not want the enemy to get between us and the sea and turn the flank of the whole British expeditionary force. But the squadron had first to find the enemy and they were never anywhere to be seen. We scoured the countryside for days before finally blundering into them – and that was a day I shall never forget, the day of our first battle.

Rumour rippled back along the column that the enemy had been sighted, a battalion of infantry on the march. They were out in the open a mile or so away, hidden from us by a long thick copse of oaks that ran alongside the road. The orders rang out: 'Forward! Form squadron column! Draw swords!' As one, the men reached down and grasped their swords from their sheaths and the air flickered with bright steel before the blades settled on the troopers' shoulders. 'Squadron, right shoulder!' came the command, and we walked in line abreast into the wood. I felt Captain Nicholls' knees close right around me and he loosened the reins. His body was taut and for the first time he felt heavy on my back. 'Easy Joey,' he said softly. 'Easy now. Don't get excited. We'll come out of this all right, don't you worry.'

I turned to look at Topthorn who was already up on his toes ready for the trot that we knew was to come. I moved instinctively closer to him and then as the bugle sounded we charged out of the shade of the wood and into the sunlight of battle.

The gentle squeak of leather, the jingling harness and the noise of hastily barked orders were drowned now by the pounding of hooves and the shout of the troopers as we galloped down on the enemy in the valley below us. Out of the corner of my eye, I was aware of the glint of Captain Nicholls' heavy sword. I felt his spurs in my side and I heard his battle cry. I saw the grey soldiers ahead of us raise their rifles and heard the death rattle of a machine-gun, and then quite suddenly I found that I had no rider, that I had no weight on my back any more and that I was alone out in front of the squadron. Topthorn was no longer beside me, but with horses behind me I knew there was only one way to gallop and that was forward. Blind terror drove me on, with my flying stirrups whipping me into a frenzy. With no rider to carry I reached the kneeling riflemen first and they scattered as I came upon them.

I ran on until I found myself alone and away from the noise of the battle, and I would never have stopped at all had I not found Topthorn once more beside me with Captain Stewart leaning over to gather up my reins before leading me back to the battlefield.

We had won, I heard it said; but horses lay dead and dying everywhere. More than a quarter of the squadron had been lost in that one action. It had all been so quick and so deadly. A cluster of grey uniformed prisoners had been taken and they huddled together now under the trees whilst the squadron regrouped and exchanged extravagant reminiscenses of a victory that had happened almost by accident rather than by design.

I never saw Captain Nicholls again and that was a great and terrible sadness for me for he had been a kind and gentle man and had cared for me well as he had promised. As I was to learn, there were few enough such good men in the world. 'He'd have been proud of you, Joey,' said Captain Stewart as he led me back to the horselines with Topthorn. 'He'd have been proud of you the way you kept going out there. He died leading that charge and you finished it for him. He'd have been proud of you.'

Topthorn stood over me that night as we bivouacked on the edge of the woods. We looked out together over the moonlit valley, and I longed for home. Only the occasional coughing and stamping of the sentries broke the still of the night. The guns were silent at last. Topthorn sank down beside me and we slept.

CHAPTER 7

IT WAS JUST AFTER REVEILLE THE NEXT MORNING and we were rummaging around in our nosebags for the last of our oats, when I saw Captain Jamie Stewart striding along the horselines towards us. Behind him, swamped in a vast greatcoat and a peaked cap, trailed a young trooper I had never seen before. He was pink-faced and young under his hat and reminded me at once of Albert. I sensed that he was nervous of me, for his approach was hesitant and reluctant.

Captain Stewart felt Topthorn's ears and stroked his soft muzzle as he always did the first thing in the morning, and then reaching across he patted me gently on the neck. 'Well Trooper Warren, here he is,' said

Captain Stewart. 'Come closer Trooper, he won't bite. This is Joey. This horse belonged to the best friend I ever had, so you look after him, d'you hear?' His tone was firm but not unsympathetic. 'And Trooper, I shall be able to keep my eye on you all the time because these two horses are inseparable. They are the two best horses in the squadron, and they know it.' He stepped closer to me and lifted my forelock clear of my face. 'Joey,' he whispered. 'You take care of him. He's only a little lad and he's had a rough ride in this war so far.'

So when the squadron moved out of the wood that morning I found I could no longer walk alongside Topthorn as I had before with Captain Nicholls, but was now just one of the troop following behind the officers in a long column of troopers. But whenever we stopped to feed or drink Trooper Warren was careful to walk me over to where Topthorn stood so that we could be together.

Trooper Warren was not a good horseman – I could tell that the minute he mounted me. He was always tense and rode me heavy in the saddle like a sack of potatoes. He had neither the experience and confidence of Corporal Samuel Perkins nor the finesse and sensitivity of Captain Nicholls. He rocked unevenly in the saddle and rode me always on too tight a rein so that I was forced to toss my head continuously to loosen it. But once out of the saddle he was the gentlest of men. He was meticulous and kind in his grooming and attended at once to my frequent and painful saddle sores, chafings and windgalls to which I was particularly prone. He cared for me as no one had since I left home. Over the next few months it was his loving attention that was to keep me alive.

There were a few minor skirmishes during that first autumn of the war, but as Captain Nicholls had predicted, we were used less and less as cavalry and more as transport for mounted infantry. Whenever we came across the enemy the squadron would dismount, drawing their rifles from their buckets, and the horses would be left behind out of sight under the care of a few troopers, so that we never saw any action ourselves but heard the distant crackle of rifle-fire and the rattle of machine-guns. When the troop returned and the squadron moved off again, there were always one or two horses without riders.

We would be on the march for hours and days on end it seemed. Then suddenly a motorcycle would roar past us through the dust and there would be the barked commands and the shrill call of the bugles and the squadron would swing off the road and into action once more.

It was during these long, stifling marches and during the cold nights that followed, that Trooper Warren began to talk to me. He told me how in the same action in which Captain Nicholls had been killed, he had had his horse shot down from beneath him and how only a few weeks before he had been an apprentice black-smith with his father. Then the war had broken out. He did not want to join up, he said; but the squire of the village had spoken to his father and his father, who rented his house and his smithy from the squire, had no option but to send him off to war, and since he had grown up around horses he volunteered to join the cavalry. 'I tell you, Joey,' he said one evening as he was picking out my hooves, 'I tell you I never thought I would get on a horse again after that first battle. Strange thing is, Joey, that it wasn't the shooting, somehow I didn't mind that; it was just the idea of riding a horse again that terrified the life out of me. Wouldn't think that possible, would you? Not with me being a smithy and all. Still, I'm over it now and you've done that for me Joey. Given me back my confidence.

Feel I can do anything now. Feel like one of those knights in armour when I'm up on you.'

Then, with the onset of winter, the rain came down in sheets. It was refreshing at first and a welcome break from the dust and the flies, but soon the fields and paths turned to mud beneath us. The squadron could no longer bivouac in the dry for there was little enough shelter and so both man and horse were constantly soaked to the skin. There was little or no protection from the driving rain, and at night we stood now over our fetlocks in cold, oozing mud. But Trooper Warren looked after me with great devotion, finding shelter for me wherever and whenever he could, rubbing some warmth into me with whisps of dry straw whenever he could find it and ensuring that I always got a good ration of oats in my nosebag to keep me going. As the weeks passed his pride in my strength and stamina became obvious to everyone, as did my affection for him. If only, I thought, if only he could just groom me and care for me and someone else could ride me.

My Trooper Warren would talk a great deal about how the war was going. We were, he said, to be withdrawn to reserve camps behind our own lines. The armies it appeared had pounded each other to a stand-still in the mud and had dug in. The dugouts had soon become trenches and the trenches had joined each other, zigzagging across the country from the sea to Switzerland. In the spring, he said, we would be needed again to break the deadlock. The cavalry could go where the infantry could not and were fast enough to overrun the trenches. We'd show the infantry how to do it, he said. But there was the winter to survive before the ground became hard enough again for the cavalry to be used effectively.

Topthorn and I spent that winter sheltering each other as best we could from the snow and the sleet, whilst only a few miles away we could hear the guns pounding each other day and night incessantly. We saw the cheery soldiers smiling under their tin hats as they marched off to the front line, whistling and singing and joking as they went, and we watched the remnants struggling back haggard and silent under their dripping capes in the rain.

Every once in a while Trooper Warren would receive a letter from home and he would read it out to me in a guarded whisper in case anyone else should overhear. The letters were all from his mother and they all said much the same thing.

'*My dear Charlie,*' he would read. '*Your Father hopes you are well and so do I. We missed having you with us at Christmas – the table in the kitchen seemed empty without you. But your little brother helps when he can with the work and Father says he's coming on well even though he's still a bit little and not strong enough yet to hold the farmhorses. Minnie Whittle, that old widow from Hanniford Farm, died in her sleep last week. She was eighty so she can't grumble at that, though I expect she would if she could. She was always the world's worst grumbler, do you remember? Well, son, that's about all our news. Your Sally from the village sends her best and says to tell you that she'll be writing soon. Keep safe, dearest boy, and come home soon.*

'*Your loving Mother.*

'But Sally won't write, Joey, because she can't, well not very well anyway. But just as soon as this lot's over and finished with I'll get back home and marry her. I've grown up with her, Joey, known her all my life. S'pose I know her almost as well as I know myself, and I like her a lot better.'

Trooper Warren broke the terrible monotony of that

winter. He lifted my spirits and I could see that Topthorn too welcomed every visit he made to the horselines. He never knew how much good he did us. During that awful winter so many of the horses went off to the veterinary hospital and never came back. Like all army horses we were clipped out like hunters so that all our lower quarters were exposed to the mud and rain. The weaker ones amongst us suffered first, for they had little resilience and went downhill fast. But Topthorn and I came through to the spring, Topthorn surviving a severe cough that shook his whole massive frame as if it was trying to tear the life out of him from the inside. It was Captain Stewart who saved him, feeding him up with a hot mash and covering him as best he could in the bleakest weather.

And then, one ice-cold night in early spring, with frost lying on our backs, the troopers came to the horselines unexpectedly early. It was before dawn. There had been a night of incessant heavy barrage. There was a new bustle and excitement in the camp. This was not one of the routine exercises we had come to expect. The troopers came along the horselines in full service order, two bandoliers, respiratory haversack, rifle and sword. We were saddled up and moved silently out of the camp and onto the road. The troopers talked of the battle ahead and all the frustrations and irritations of imposed idleness vanished as they sang in the saddle. And my Trooper Warren was singing along with them as lustily as any of them. In the cold grey of the night the squadron joined the regiment in the remnants of a little ruined village peopled only by cats, and waited there for an hour until the pale light of dawn crept over the horizon. Still the guns bellowed out their fury and the ground shook beneath us. We passed the field hospitals and the light guns before trotting over the support trenches to catch our first sight of the battle-field. Desolation and destruction were everywhere. Not a building was left intact. Not a blade of grass grew in the torn and ravaged soil. The singing around me stopped and we moved on in ominous silence and out over the trenches that were crammed with men, their bayonets fixed to their rifles. They gave us a sporadic cheer as we clattered over the boards and out into the wilderness of no man's land, into a wilderness of wire and shell holes and the terrible litter of war. Suddenly the guns stopped firing overhead. We were through the wire. The squadron fanned out in a wide, uneven echelon and the bugle sounded. I felt the spurs biting into my sides and moved up alongside Topthorn as we broke into a trot. 'Do me proud, Joey,' said Trooper Warren, drawing his sword. 'Do me proud.'

CHAPTER 8

FOR JUST A FEW SHORT MOMENTS WE MOVED forward at the trot as we had done in training. In the eery silence of no man's land all that could be heard was the jingle of the harness and the snorting of the horses. We picked our way around the craters keeping our line as best we could. Up ahead of us at the top of a gentle sloping hill were the battered remnants of a wood and just below a hideous, rusting roll of barbed wire that stretched out along the horizon as far as the eye could see.

'Wire,' I heard Trooper Warren whisper through his teeth. 'Oh God, Joey, they said the wire would be gone, they said the guns would deal with the wire. Oh my God!'

We were into a canter now and still there was no sound nor sight of any enemy. The troopers were shouting at an invisible foe, leaning over their horses' necks, their sabres stretched out in front of them. I galvanised myself into a gallop to keep with Topthorn and as I did, so the first terrible shells fell amongst us and the machine guns opened up. The bedlam of battle had begun. All around me men cried and fell to the ground, and horses reared and screamed in an agony of fear and pain. The ground erupted on either side of me, throwing horses and riders clear into the air. The shells whined and roared overhead, and every explosion seemed like an earthquake to us. But the squadron galloped on inexorably through it all towards the wire at the top of the hill, and I went with them.

On my back Trooper Warren held me in an iron grip with his knees. I stumbled once and felt him lose a stirrup, and slowed so that he could find it again. Topthorn was still ahead of me, his head up, his tail whisking from side to side. I found more strength in my legs and charged after him. Trooper Warren prayed aloud as he rode, but his prayers turned soon to curses as he saw the carnage around him. Only a few horses reached the wire and Topthorn and I were amongst them. There were indeed a few holes blasted through the wire by our bombardment so that some of us could find a way through; and we came at last upon the first line of enemy trenches, but they were empty. The firing came now from higher up in amongst the trees; and so the squadron, or what was left of it, regrouped and galloped up into the wood, only to be met by a line of hidden wire in amongst the trees. Some of the horses ran into the wire before they could be stopped, and stuck there, their riders trying feverishly to extract them. I saw one trooper dismount deliberately once he saw his horse was caught. He pulled out his rifle and shot his mount before falling dead himself on the wire. I could see at once that there was no way through, that the only way was to jump the wire and when I saw Topthorn and Captain Stewart leap over where the wire was lowest, I followed them and we found ourselves at last in amongst the enemy. From behind every tree, from trenches all around it seemed, they ran forward in their piked helmets to counter-attack. They rushed past us, ignoring us until we found ourselves surrounded by an entire company of soldiers, their rifles pointing up at us.

The crump of the shelling and the spitting of rifle-fire

had suddenly stopped. I looked around me for the rest of the squadron, to discover that we were alone. Behind us the riderless horses, all that was left of a proud cavalry squadron, galloped back towards our trenches, and the hillside below was strewn with the dead and dying.

'Throw down your sword, Trooper,' said Captain Stewart, bending in his saddle and dropping his sword to the ground. 'There's been enough useless slaughter today. No sense in adding to it.' He walked Topthorn closer towards us and reined in. 'Trooper, I told you once we had the best horses in the squadron, and today they showed us they are the best horses in the entire regiment, in the whole confounded army – and there's not a scratch on them.' He dismounted as the German soldiers closed in and Trooper Warren followed suit. They stood side by side holding our reins while we were surrounded. We looked back down the hill at the battle-field. A few horses were still struggling on the wire, but one by one they were put out of their misery by the advancing German infantry, who had already regained their line of trenches. They were the last shots in the battle.

'What a waste,' the Captain said. 'What a ghastly

waste. Maybe now when they see this they'll understand that you can't send horses into wire and
machine-guns. Maybe now they'll think again.'

The soldiers around us seemed wary of us and kept
their distance. They seemed not to know quite what to
do with us. 'The horses, sir?' Trooper Warren asked.
'Joey and Topthorn, what happens to them now?'

'Same as us, Trooper,' said Captain Stewart. 'They're
prisoners of war just as we are.' Flanked by the soldiers
who hardly spoke, we were escorted over the brow of
a hill and down into the valley below. Here the valley
was still green for there had been no battle over this
ground as yet. All the while Trooper Warren had his
arm over my neck to reassure me and I felt then that
he was beginning to say goodbye.

He spoke softly into my ear. 'Don't suppose they'll
let you come with me where I'm going, Joey. I wish
they could, but they can't. But I shan't ever forget you.
I promise you that.'

'Don't you worry, Trooper,' Captain Stewart said.
'The Germans love their horses every bit as much as we
do. They'll be all right. Anyway, Topthorn will look
after your Joey – you can be sure of that.'

As we came out of the wood and onto the road

below we were halted by our escort. Captain Stewart and Trooper Warren were marched away down the road towards a cluster of ruined buildings that must at one time have been a village, whilst Topthorn and I were led away across the fields and further down the valley. There was no time for long farewells – just a brief last stroke of the muzzle for each of us and they were gone. As they walked away, Captain Stewart had his arm around Trooper Warren's shoulder.

CHAPTER 9

WE WERE LED AWAY BY TWO NERVOUS SOLDIERS down farm tracks, through orchards and across a bridge before being tied up beside a hospital tent some miles from where we had been captured. A knot of wounded soldiers gathered around us at once. They patted and stroked us and I began to whisk my tail with impatience. I was hungry and thirsty and angry that I had been separated from my Trooper Warren.

Still no one seemed to know quite what to do with us until an officer in a long grey coat with a bandage round his head emerged from the tent. He was an immensely tall man standing a full head higher than anyone around him. The manner of his gait and the way he held himself indicated a man clearly accustomed to wielding authority. A bandage came down over one eye so that he had only half a face visible. As he walked towards us I saw that he was limping, that one foot was heavily bandaged and that he needed the support of a stick. The soldiers sprang back at his approach and stood stiffly to attention. He looked us both over in undisguised admiration, shaking his head and sighing as he did so. Then he turned to the men. 'There are hundreds like these dead out on our wire. I tell you, if we had had one jot of the courage of these animals we should be in Paris by now and not slugging it out here in the mud. These two horses came through hell-fire to get here – they were the only two to make it. It was not their fault they were sent on a fool's errand. They are not circus animals, they are heroes, do you understand, heroes, and they should be treated as such. And you stand around and gawp at them. You are none of you badly wounded and the doctor is far too busy to see you at present. So, I want these horses unsaddled, rubbed down, fed and watered at once. They will need oats and hay, and a blanket for each of them, now get moving.'

The soldiers hurried away, scattering in all directions,

and within a few minutes Topthorn and I were being lavished with all manner of clumsy kindness. None of them had handled a horse before it seemed, but that did not matter to us so grateful were we for all the fodder they brought us and the water. We lacked for nothing that morning, and all the time the tall officer supervised from under the trees, leaning on his stick. From time to time he would come up to us and run his hand along our backs and over our quarters, nodding his approval and lecturing his men on the finer points of horse breeding as he examined us. After a time he was joined by a man in a white coat who emerged from the tent, his hair dishevelled, his face pale with exhaustion. There was blood on his coat.

'Headquarters phoned through about the horses, Herr Hauptmann,' said the man in white. 'And they say I am to keep them for the stretcher cases. I know your views on the matter Hauptmann, but I'm afraid you cannot have them. We need them here desperately, and the way things are going I fear we will need more. That was just the first attack – there will be more to come. We expect a sustained offensive – it will be a long battle. We are the same on both sides, once we start something we seem to have to prove a point and that takes time and lives. We'll need all the ambulance transport we can get, motorised or horse.'

The tall officer drew himself up to his full height, and bristled with indignation. He was a formidable sight as he advanced on the man in white. 'Doctor, you cannot put fine British cavalry horses to pulling carts! Any of our horse regiments, my own Regiment of Lancers indeed, would be proud, indeed overwhelmed to have such splendid creatures in their ranks. You cannot do it, Doctor, I will not permit it.'

'Herr Hauptmann,' said the doctor patiently – he was clearly not at all intimidated. 'Do you really imagine that after this morning's madness that either side will be using cavalry again in this war? Can you not understand that we need transport, Herr Hauptmann? And we need it now. There are men, brave men, German and English lying out there on stretchers in the trenches and at present there's not enough transport to bring them back to the hospital here. Now do you want them all to die, Herr Hauptmann? Tell me that. Do you want them to die? If these horses could be hitched up to a cart they could bring them back in their dozens. We just do not have enough ambulances to cope, and what we do have break down or get stuck in the mud. Please, Herr Hauptmann. We need your help.'

'The world,' said the German officer, shaking his head, 'the world has gone quite mad. When noble creatures such as these are forced to become beasts of burden, the world has gone mad. But I can see that you are right. I am a lancer, Herr Doctor, but even I know that men are more important than horses. But you must see to it that you have someone in charge of these two who knows horses – I don't want any dirty-fingered mechanic getting his hands on these two. And you must tell them that they are riding horses. They won't take kindly to pulling carts, no matter how noble the cause.'

'Thank you, Herr Hauptmann,' said the doctor. 'You are most kind, but I have a problem Herr Hauptmann. As I am sure you will agree, they will need an expert to manage them to start with, particularly if they have never been put in a cart before. The problem is that I have only medical orderlies here. True, one of them has worked horses on a farm before the war; but to tell you the truth, Herr Hauptmann, I have no one who could manage these two – no one that is except you. You are due to go to Base Hospital on the next convoy of ambulances, but they won't be here before this evening. I know it's a lot to ask of a wounded man, but you can see how desperate I am. The farmer down below has several carts, and I should imagine all the harness you would need. What do you say, Herr Hauptmann? Can you help me?'

The bandaged officer limped back towards us and stroked our noses tenderly. Then he smiled and nodded. 'Very well. It's a sacrilege, Doctor, a sacrilege,' he said. 'But if it's got to be done, then I'd rather do it myself and see it is done properly.'

So that same afternoon after our capture, Topthorn and I were hitched up side by side to an old hay cart and with the officer directing two orderlies, we were driven up through the woods back towards the thunder of the gunfire and the wounded that awaited us. Topthorn was all the time in a great state of alarm for it was clear he had never pulled before in his life; and at last I was able in my turn to help him, to lead, to compensate and to reassure him. The officer led us at first, limping along beside me with his stick, but he was soon confident enough to mount the cart with the two orderlies and take the reins. 'You've done a bit of this before, my friend,' he said. 'I can tell that. I always knew the British were mad. Now I know that they use horses such as you as cart-horses, I am quite sure of it. That's what this war is all about, my friend. It's about which of us is the madder. And clearly you British started with an advantage. You were mad beforehand.'

All that afternoon and evening while the battle raged we trudged up to the lines, loaded up with the stretcher cases and brought them back to the Field Hospital. It was several miles each way over roads and tracks filled with shell holes and littered with the corpses of mules and men. The artillery barrage from both sides was continuous. It roared overhead all day as the armies hurled their men at each other across no man's land, and the wounded that could walk poured back along the roads. I had seen the same grey faces looking out from under their helmets somewhere before. All that was different were the uniforms – they were grey now with red piping, and the helmets were no longer round with a broad brim.

It was almost night before the tall officer left us, waving goodbye to us and to the doctor from the back of the ambulance as it bumped its way across the field and out of sight. The doctor turned to the orderlies who had been with us all day. 'See to it that they are well cared for, those two,' he said. 'They saved good lives today, those two – good German lives and good English lives. They deserve the best of care. See to it that they have it.'

For the first time that night since we came to the war, Topthorn and I had the luxury of a stable. The shed in the farm that lay across the fields from the hospital was emptied of pigs and poultry and we were led in to find a rack brimming full with sweet hay and buckets of soothing, cold water.

That night after we had finished our hay, Topthorn and I were lying down together at the back of the shed. I was half awake and could think only of my aching muscles and sore feet. Suddenly the door creaked open and the stable filled with a flickering orange light. Behind the light there were footsteps. We looked up and I was seized at that moment with a kind of panic. For a fleeting moment I imagined myself back at home in the stable with old Zoey. The dancing light triggered off an alarm in me, reminding me at once of Albert's father. I was on my feet in an instant and backing away from the light with Topthorn beside me, protecting me. However, when the voice spoke it was not the rasping, drunken voice of Albert's father, but rather a soft, gentle tone of a girl's voice, a young girl. I could see now that there were two people behind the light, an old man, a bent old man in rough clothes and clogs, and beside him stood a young girl, her head and shoulders wrapped in a shawl.

'There you are, Grandpapa,' she said. 'I told you they put them in here. Have you ever seen anything so beautiful? Oh can they be mine, Grandpapa? Please can they be mine?'

CHAPTER 10

IF IT IS POSSIBLE TO BE HAPPY IN THE MIDDLE OF a nightmare, then Topthorn and I were happy that summer. Every day we had to make the same hazardous journeys up to the front line which in spite of almost continuous offensives and counter-offensives moved only a matter of a few hundred yards in either direction. Hauling our ambulance cart of dying and wounded back from the trenches we became a familiar sight along the pitted track. More than once we were cheered by marching soldiers as they passed us. Once, after we had plodded on, too tired to be fearful, through a devastating barrage that straddled the road in front of us and behind us, one of the soldiers with his tunic covered in blood and mud, came and stood by my head and threw his good arm around my neck and kissed me.

'Thank you, my friend,' he said. 'I never thought they would get us out of that hell-hole. I found this yesterday, and thought about keeping it for myself, but I know where it belongs.' And he reached up and hung a muddied ribbon around my neck. There was an Iron Cross dangling on the end of it. 'You'll have to share it with your friend,' he said. 'They tell me you're both English. I bet you are the first English in this war to win an Iron Cross, and the last I shouldn't wonder.' The waiting wounded outside the hospital tent clapped and cheered us to the echo, bringing doctors, nurses and patients running out of the tent to see what there could be to clap about in the midst of all this misery.

They hung our Iron Cross on a nail outside our stable door and on the rare quiet days, when the shelling stopped and we were not needed to make the journey up to the front, a few of the walking wounded would wander down from the hospital to the farmyard to visit us. I was puzzled by this adulation but loved it, thrusting my head over the high stable door whenever I heard them coming into the yard. Side by side Topthorn and I would stand at the door to receive our unlimited ration of compliments and adoration – and of course this was sometimes accompanied by a welcome gift of perhaps a lump of sugar or an apple.

But it was the evenings of that summer that stay so strong in my memory. Often it would not be until dusk that we would clatter into the yard; and there, always waiting by the stable door would be the little girl and her grandfather who had come to us that first evening. The orderlies simply handed us over into their charge – and that was just as well, for kind as they were they had no notion about horses. It was little Emilie and her grandfather who insisted that they should look after us. They rubbed us down and saw to our sores and bruises. They fed us, watered us and groomed us and somehow always found enough straw for a dry warm bed. Emilie made us each a fringe to tie over our eyes to keep the flies from bothering us, and in the warm summer evenings she would lead us out to graze in the meadow below the farmhouse and stayed with us watching us grazing until her grandfather called us in again.

She was a tiny, frail creature, but led us about the farm with complete confidence, chatting all the while about what she had been doing all the day and about how brave we were and how proud she was of us.

As winter came on again and the grass lost its flavour and goodness, she would climb up into the loft above the stable and throw down our hay for us, and she would lie down on the loft floor looking at us through the trapdoor while we pulled the hay from the rack and ate it. Then with her grandfather busying himself about us she would prattle on merrily about how when she was older and stronger and when the soldiers had all gone home and the war was over she would ride us herself through the woods – one at a time, she said – and how we would never want for anything if only we would stay with her for ever.

Topthorn and I were by now seasoned campaigners, and it may well have been that that drove us on out through the roar of the shell-fire back towards the trenches each morning, but there was more to it than that. For us it was the hope that we would be back that evening in our stable and that little Emilie would be there to comfort and to love us. We had that to look forward to and to long for. Any horse has an instinctive fondness for children for they speak more softly, and their size precludes any threat; but Emilie was a special child for us, for she spent every minute she could with us and lavished us with her affection. She would be up late every evening with us rubbing us down and seeing to our feet, and be up again at dawn to see us fed properly before the orderlies led us away and hitched us up to the ambulance cart. She would climb the wall by the pond and stand there waving, and although I could never turn round, I knew she would stay there until the road took us out of sight. And then she would be there when we came back in the evening, clasping her hands in excitement as she watched us being unhitched.

But one evening at the onset of winter she was not there to greet us as usual. We had been worked even harder that day than usual, for the first snows of winter had blocked the road up to the trenches to all but the horse-drawn vehicles and we had to make twice the number of trips to bring in the wounded. Exhausted, hungry and thirsty we were led into our stable by Emilie's grandfather, who said not a word but saw to us quickly before hurrying back across the yard to the house. Topthorn and I spent that evening by the stable door watching the gentle fall of snow and the flickering light in the farmhouse. We knew something was wrong before the old man came back and told us.

He came late at night, his feet crumping the snow. He had made up the buckets of hot mash we had come to expect and he sat down on the straw beneath the lantern and watched us eat. 'She prays for you,' he said, nodding slowly. 'Do you know, every night before she goes to bed she prays for you? I've heard her. She prays for her dead father and mother – they were killed only a week after the war began. One shell, that's all it takes. And she prays for her brother that she'll never see again – just seventeen and he doesn't even have a grave. It's as if he never lived except in our minds. Then she prays for me and for the war to pass by the farm and to leave us alone, and last of all she prays for you two. She prays for two things: first that you both survive the war and live on into ripe old age, and secondly that if you do she dearly wants to be there to be with you. She's barely thirteen, my Emilie, and now she's lying up there in her room and I don't know if she'll live to see the morning. The German doctor from the hospital tells me it's pneumonia. He's a good enough doctor even if he is German – he's done his best, it's up to God now, and so far God hasn't done too well for my family. If she goes, if my Emilie dies, then the only light left in my life will be put out.' He looked up at us through heavily wrinkled eyes and wiped the tears from his face. 'If you can understand anything of what I said, then pray for her to whatever Horse God you pray to, pray for her like she does for you.'

There was heavy shelling all that night, and before dawn the next day the orderlies came for us and led us out into the snow to be hitched up. There was no sign of Emilie nor her grandfather. Pulling the cart through the fresh, uncut snow that morning, Topthorn and I needed all our strength just to haul the empty cart up to the front line. The snow disguised perfectly the ruts and shell holes, so that we found ourselves straining to extricate ourselves from the piled-up snow and the sinking mud beneath it.

We made it to the front line, but only with the help of the two orderlies, who jumped out whenever we were in difficulties and turned the wheels over by hand until we were free again and the cart could gather momentum through the snow once more.

The field dressing station behind the front line was crowded with wounded and we had to bring back a heavier load than we ever had before, but fortunately the way back was mostly downhill. Someone suddenly remembered it was Christmas morning, and they sang slow tuneful carols all the way back. For the most part they were casualties blinded by gas and in their pain some of them cried, as they sang, for their lost sight. We made so many journeys that day and stopped only when the hospital could take no more.

It was already a starry night by the time we reached the farm. The shelling had stopped. There were no flares to light up the sky and blot out the stars. All the way along the lane not a gun fired. Peace had come for one night, one at least. The snow in the yard was crisped by the frost. There was a dancing light in our stable and Emilie's grandfather came out into the snow and took our reins from the orderly.

'It's a fine night,' he said to us as he led us in. 'It's a fine night and all's well. There's mash and hay and water in there for you – I've given you extra tonight, not because it's cold but because you prayed. You must have prayed to that Horse God of yours because my Emilie woke up at lunchtime, sat up she did, and do you know the first thing she said? I'll tell you. She said, "I must get up, got to get their mash ready for them when they come back. They'll be cold and tired," she said. The only way that German doctor could get her to stay in bed was to promise you extra rations tonight, and she made him promise to go on with them as long as the cold weather lasted. So go inside my beauties and eat your fill. We've all had a Christmas present today, haven't we? All's well, I tell you. All's well.'

CHAPTER 11

AND ALL WAS TO STAY WELL FOR A TIME AT LEAST. For the war suddenly moved away from us that spring. We knew it was not over for we could still hear distant thunder of the guns and the troops came marching through the farmyard from time to time up towards the line. But there were fewer wounded now to bring in and we were needed less and less to pull our ambulance cart back and forth from the trenches. Topthorn and I were put out to grass in the meadow by the pond most days, but the evenings were still cold with the occasional frost and our Emilie would always come to get us in before dark. She did not need to lead us. She had but to call and we followed.

Emilie was still weak from her illness and coughed a great deal as she fussed around us in the stable. From time to time now she would heave herself up on to my back and I would walk so gently around the yard and out into the meadow with Topthorn following close behind. She used no reins on me, no saddle, no bits, no spurs, and sat astride me not as my mistress but rather as a friend. Topthorn was just that much taller and broader than me and she found it very difficult to mount him and even more difficult to get down. Sometimes she would use me as a stepping-stone to Topthorn, but it was a difficult manoeuvre for her and more than once she fell off in the attempt.

But between Topthorn and me there was never any jealousy and he was quite content to plod around beside us and take her on board whenever she felt like it. One evening we were out in the meadow sheltering under the chestnut tree from the heat of the new summer sun when we heard the sound of an approaching convoy of lorries coming back from the front. As they came through the farm gate they called out to us and we recognised them as the orderlies, nurses and doctors from the field hospital. As the convoy stopped in the yard we galloped over to the gate by the pond and looked over. Emilie and her grandfather emerged from the milking shed and were deep in conversation with the doctor. Quite suddenly we found ourselves besieged by all the orderlies we had come to know so well. They climbed the fence and patted and smoothed us with great affection. They were exuberant yet somehow sad at the same time. Emilie was running over towards us shouting and screaming.

'I knew it would happen,' she said. 'I knew it. I prayed for it to happen and it did happen. They don't need you any more to pull their carts. They're moving the hospital further up along the valley. There's a big, big battle going on up there and so they're moving away from us. But they don't want to take you with them. That kind doctor has told Grandpapa that you can both stay – it's a kind of payment for the cart they used and the food they took and because we looked after you throughout all the winter. He says you can stay and work on the farm until the army needs you again – and they never will, and if they ever did I'd hide you. We'll never let them take you away, will we, Grandpapa? Never, never.'

And so after the long, sad farewells the convoy moved away up the road in a cloud of dust and we were left alone and in peace with Emilie and her grand-father. The peace was to prove sweet but short-lived.

To my great delight I found myself once more a farm horse. With Topthorn harnessed up beside me we set to work the very next day cutting and turning the hay. When Emilie protested, after that first long day in the fields, that her grandfather was working us too hard, he put his hands on her shoulders and said, 'Nonsense Emilie. They like to work. They need to work. And besides the only way for us to go on living, Emilie, is to go on like we did before. The soldiers have gone now so if we pretend hard enough then maybe the war will go away altogether. We must live as we have always lived, cutting our hay, picking our apples and tilling our soil. We cannot live as if there will be no tomorrow. We can live only if we eat, and our food comes from the land. We must work the land if we want to live and these two must work it with us. They don't mind, they like the work. Look at them, Emilie, do they look unhappy?'

For Topthorn the transition from pulling an ambu-lance cart to pulling a hay turner was not a difficult one and he adapted easily; and for me it was a dream I had dreamed many times since I had left the farm in Devon.

I was working once more with happy, laughing people around me who cared for me. We pulled with a will that harvest, Topthorn and I, hauling in the heavy hay wagons to the barns where Emilie and her grandfather would unload. And Emilie continued to watch over us lovingly – every scratch and bruise was tended to at once and her grandfather was never allowed to work us for too long however much he argued. But the return to the peaceful life of a farm horse could not last long, not in the middle of that war.

The hay was almost all gathered in when the soldiers came back again one evening. We were in our stables when we heard the sound of approaching hoofbeats and the rumbling of wheels on the cobble-stones as the column came trotting into the yard. The horses, six at a time, were yoked to great heavy guns, and they stood in their traces puffing and blowing with exertion. Each pair was ridden by men whose faces were severe and hard under their grey caps. I noticed at once that these were not the gentle orderlies that had left us only a few short weeks before. Their faces were strange and harsh and there was a new alarm and urgency in their eyes. Few of them seemed to laugh or even smile. These were a different breed of men from those we had seen before. Only one old soldier who drove the ammunition cart came over to stroke us and spoke kindly to little Emilie.

After a brief consultation with Emilie's grandfather the artillery troop bivouacked in our meadow that night, watering the horses in our pond. Topthorn and I were excited by the arrival of new horses and spent all evening with our heads over the stable door neighing to them, but most of them seemed too tired to reply. Emilie came to tell us about the soldiers that evening and we could see she was worried for she would talk only a whisper.

'Grandpapa doesn't like them here,' she said. 'He doesn't trust the officer, says he's got eyes like a wasp and you can't trust a wasp. But they'll be gone in the morning, then we'll be on our own again.'

Early that next morning, as the dark of night left the sky, a visitor came to our stables. It was a pale, thin man in dusty uniform who peered over the door to inspect us. He had eyes that stood out of his face in a permanent stare and he wore a pair of wire-framed spectacles through which he watched us intently, nodding as he did so. He stood a few minutes and then left.

By full light the artillery troop was drawn up in the

yard and ready to move, there was a loud and incessant knocking on the farmhouse door and we saw Emilie and her grandfather come out into the yard still dressed in their night-clothes. 'Your horses, Monsieur,' the bespectacled officer announced baldly, 'I shall be taking your horses with us. I have one team with only four horses and I need two more. They look fine, strong animals and they will learn quickly. We will be taking them with us.'

'But how can I work my farm without horses?' Emilie's grandfather said. 'They are just farm horses, they won't be able to pull guns.'

'Sir,' said the officer, 'there is a war on and I have to have horses for my guns. I have to take them. What you do on your farm is your own business, but I must have the horses. The army needs them.'

'But you can't,' Emilie cried. 'They're my horses. You can't take them. Don't let them, Grandpapa, don't let them, please don't let them.'

The old man shrugged his shoulders sadly. 'My child,' he said quietly. 'What can I do? How could I stop them? Do you suggest I cut them to pieces with my scythe, or lay about them with my axe? No my child, we knew it might happen one day, didn't we? We talked about it often enough, didn't we? We knew they would go one day. Now I want no tears in front of these people. You're to be proud and strong like your brother was and I'll not have you weaken in front of them. Go and say your good-byes to the horses, Emilie, and be brave.'

Little Emilie led us to the back of the stable and slipped our halters on, carefully arranging our manes so that they were not snagged by the rope. Then she reached up and put her arms about us, leaning her head into each of us in turn and crying softly. 'Come back,' she said. 'Please come back to me. I shall die if you don't come back.' She wiped her eyes and pushed back her hair before opening the stable door and leading us out into the yard. She walked us directly towards the officer and handed over the reins. 'I want them back,' she said, her voice strong now, almost fierce. 'I'm just lending them to you. They are my horses. They belong here. Feed them well and look after them and make sure you bring them back.' And she walked past her grandfather and into the house without even turning round.

As we left the farm, hauled unwillingly along behind the ammunition cart, I turned and saw Emilie's grandfather still standing in the yard. He was smiling and waving at us through his tears. Then the rope jerked my neck violently around and jolted me into a trot, and I recalled the time once before when I had been roped up to a cart and dragged away against my will. But at least this time I had my Topthorn with me.

CHAPTER 12

PERHAPS IT WAS THE CONTRAST WITH THE FEW idyllic months we had spent with Emilie and her grandfather that made what followed so harsh and so bitter an experience for Topthorn and me; or perhaps it was just that the war was all the time becoming more terrible. In places now the guns were lined up only a few yards apart for miles and miles and when they sounded out their fury the very earth shook beneath us. The lines of wounded seemed interminable now and the countryside was laid waste for miles behind the trenches.

The work itself was certainly no harder than when we had been pulling the ambulance cart, but now we were no longer stabled every night, and of course we no longer had the protection of our Emilie to rely on. Suddenly the war was no longer distant. We were back amongst the fearful noise and stench of battle, hauling our gun through the mud, urged on and sometimes whipped on by men who displayed little care or interest in our welfare just so long as we got the guns where they had to go. It was not that they were cruel men, but just that they seemed to be driven now by a fearful compulsion that left no room and no time for pleasantness or consideration either for each other or for us.

Food was scarcer now. We received our corn ration only spasmodically as winter came on again and there was only a meagre hay ration for each of us. One by one we began to lose weight and condition. At the same time the battles seemed to become more furious and prolonged and we worked longer and harder hours pulling in front of the gun; we were permanently sore and permanently cold. We ended every day covered in a layer of cold, dripping mud that seemed to seep through and chill us to the bones.

The gun team was a motley collection of six horses. Of the four we joined only one had the height and the strength to pull as a gun horse should, a great hulk of a horse they called Heinie who seemed quite unperturbed by all that was going on around him. The rest of the team tried to live up to his example, but only Topthorn succeeded. Heinie and Topthorn were the leading pair, and I found myself in the traces behind Topthorn next to a thin, wiry little horse they called Coco. He had a display of white patch-marks over his face that often caused amusement amongst the soldiers as we passed by. But there was nothing funny about Coco – he had the nastiest temper of any horse I had ever met, either before or since. When Coco was eating no one, neither horse nor man, ventured within biting or kicking distance. Behind us was a perfectly matched pair of smaller dun-coloured ponies with flaxen manes and tails. No one could tell them apart, even the soldiers referred to them not by name but merely as 'the two golden Haflingers'. Because they were pretty and invariably friendly they received much attention and even a little affection from the gunners. They must have been an incongruous but cheering sight to the tired soldiers as we trotted through the ruined villages up to the front. There was no doubt that they worked as hard as the rest of us and that in spite of their diminutive size they were at least our equals in stamina; but in the canter they acted as a brake, slowed us down and spoiled the rhythm of the team.

Strangely enough it was the giant Heinie who showed the first signs of weakness. The cold sinking mud and the lack of proper fodder through that appalling winter began to shrink his massive frame and reduced him within months to a poor, skinny looking creature. So to my delight – and I must confess it – they moved me up into the leading pair with Topthorn; and Heinie dropped back now to pull alongside little Coco who had begun the ordeal with little strength in reserve. They both went rapidly downhill until the two of them were only any use for pulling on flat, hard surfaces, and since we scarcely ever travelled over such ground they were soon of little use in the team, and made the work for the rest of us that much more arduous.

Each night we spent in the lines up to our hocks in freezing mud, in conditions far worse than that first winter of the war when Topthorn and I had been cavalry horses. Then each horse had had a trooper who did all he could to care for us and comfort us, but now the efficiency of the gun was the first priority and we came a very poor second. We were mere work horses, and treated as such. The gunners themselves were grey in the face with exhaustion and hunger. Survival was all that mattered to them now. Only the kind old gunner I had noticed that first day when we were taken from the farm seemed to have the time to stay with us. He fed us with hard bits of crumbly black bread and spent more time with us than with his fellow soldiers whom he seemed to avoid all he could. He was an untidy, portly little man who chuckled incessantly and would talk more to himself than to anyone else.

The effects of continual exposure, under-feeding and hard work were now apparent in all of us. Few of us had any hair growing on our lower legs and the skin below was a mass of cracked sores. Even the rugged little Haflingers began to lose condition. Like all the others I found every step I took now excruciatingly painful particularly in my forelegs which were cracking badly from the knees downwards, and there was not a horse in the team that was not walking lame. The vets treated us as best they could, and even the most hard-hearted of the gunners seemed disturbed as our condition worsened, but there was nothing anyone could do until the mud disappeared.

The field vets shook their heads in despair, and pulled back those they could for rest and recuperation; but some had deteriorated so much that they were led away and shot there and then after the vet's inspection. Heinie went that way one morning, and we passed him lying in the mud, a collapsed wreck of a horse; and so eventually did Coco who was hit in his neck by flying shrapnel and had to be destroyed where he lay by the side of the road. No matter how much I disliked him – and he was a vicious beast – it was a piteous and terrible sight to see a fellow creature with whom I had pulled for so long, discarded and forgotten in a ditch.

The little Haflingers stayed with us all through the winter straining their broad backs and pulling against the traces with all the strength they could muster. They were both gentle and kind, with not a shred of aggression in their courageous souls, and Topthorn and I came to love them dearly. In their turn they looked up to us for support and friendship and we gave both willingly.

I first noticed that Topthorn was failing when I felt the gun pulling more heavily than before. We were fording a small stream when the wheels of the gun became stuck in the mud. I turned quickly to look at him and saw him suddenly labouring and low in his stride. His eyes told me the pain he was suffering and I pulled all the harder to enable him to ease up.

That night with the rain sheeting down relentlessly on our backs I stood over him as he lay down in the mud. He lay not on his stomach as he always did, but stretched out on his side, lifting his head from time to time as spasms of coughing shook him. He coughed intermittently all night and slept only fitfully. I worried over him, nuzzling him and licking him to try to keep him warm and to reassure him that he was not alone in his pain. I consoled myself with the thought that no horse I had ever seen had the power and stamina of Topthorn and that he must have a reservoir of great strength to fall back on in his sickness.

And sure enough he was up on his feet the next morning before the gunners came to feed us our ration of corn, and although his head hung lower than usual and he moved only ponderously, I could see that he had the strength to survive if only he could rest.

I noticed however that when the vet came that day checking along the lines, he looked long and hard at Topthorn and listened carefully to his chest. 'He's a strong one,' I heard him tell the spectacled officer – a man whom no one liked, neither horses nor men. 'There's fine breeding here, too fine perhaps Herr Major, could well be his undoing. He's too fine to pull a gun. I'd pull him out, but you have no horse to take his place, have you? He'll go on I suppose, but go easy on him, Herr Major. Take the team as slow as you can, else you'll have no team, and without your team your gun won't be a lot of use, will it?'

'He will have to do what the others do, Herr Doctor,' said the major in a steely voice. 'No more and no less. I cannot make exceptions. If you pass him fit, he's fit and that's that.'

'He's fit to go on,' said the vet reluctantly. 'But I am warning you Herr Major. You must take care.'

'We do what we can,' said the major dismissively. And to be fair they did. It was the mud that was killing us one by one, the mud, the lack of shelter and the lack of food.

CHAPTER 13

SO TOPTHORN CAME INTO THAT SPRING WEAKENED severely by his illness and still with a husky cough, but he had survived. We had both survived. There was hard ground to go on now, and the grass grew once more in the fields so that out bodies began to fill out again, and our coats lost their winter raggedness and shone in the sun. The sun shone too on the soldiers, whose uniforms of grey and red stayed cleaner. They shaved more often now, and they began as they always did every spring to talk of the end of the war and about home and about how the next attack would finish it and how they would see their families again soon. They were happier and so they treated us that much better.

The rations improved too with the weather and our gun-team stepped out with a new enthusiasm and purpose. The sores disappeared from our legs and we had full bellies each day, all the grass we could eat and oats in plenty.

The two little Haflingers puffed and snorted behind us, and they shamed Topthorn and me into a gallop – something we had not been able to achieve all winter no matter how hard our riders tried to whip us on. Our new-found health and the optimism of the singing, whistling soldiers brought us to a fresh sense of exhilaration as we rolled our guns along the pitted roads into position.

But there were to be no battles for us that summer. There was always sporadic firing and shelling but the armies seemed content to growl at each other and threaten without ever coming to grips. Further away of course we heard the renewed fury of the spring offensive up and down the line, but we were not needed to move our guns and spent that summer in comparative peace some way behind the lines. Idleness, even boredom set in as we grazed the lush buttercup meadows and we even became fat for the first time since we came to war. Perhaps it was because we became too fat that

Topthorn and I were chosen to pull the ammunition cart from the railhead some miles away up to the artillery lines, and so we found ourselves under the command of the kind old soldier who had been so good to us all winter.

Everyone called him mad old Friedrich. He was thought to be mad because he talked continuously to himself and even when he was not talking he was laughing and chortling at some private joke that he never shared with anyone. Mad old Friedrich was the old soldier they set to work on tasks no one else wanted to do because he was always obliging and everyone knew it.

In the heat and the dust it was tedious and strenuous work that quickly took off our excess weight and began to sap our strength once more. The cart was always too heavy for us to pull because they insisted at the railhead on filling it up with as many shells as possible in spite of Friedrich's protestations. They simply laughed at him, ignored him and piled on the shells. On the way back to the artillery lines Friedrich would always walk up the hills, leading us slowly for he knew how heavy the wagon must have been. We stopped often for rests and for water and he made quite sure that we had more food than the other horses who were resting all that summer.

We came to look forward now to each morning when Friedrich would come to fetch us in from the field, put on our harness and we would leave the noise and the bustle of the camp behind us. We soon discovered that Friedrich was not in the slightest bit mad, but simply a kind and gentle man whose whole nature cried out against fighting a war. He confessed to us as we plodded along the road to the railhead that he longed only to be back in his butcher's shop in Schleiden, and that he talked to himself because he felt that he was the only one who understood himself or would even listen to what he was saying. He laughed to himself he said because if he did not laugh he would cry.

'I tell you, my friends,' he said one day. 'I tell you that I am the only sane man in the regiment. It's the others that are mad, but they don't know it. They fight a war and they don't know what for. Isn't that crazy? How can one man kill another and not really know the reason why he does it, except that the other man wears a different colour uniform and speaks a different language? And it's me they call mad! You two are the only rational creatures I've met in this benighted war, and like me the only reason you're here is because you were brought here. If I had the courage – and I haven't – we'd take off down this road and never come back. But then they'd shoot me when they caught me and my wife and my children and my mother and my father would have the shame of it on them for ever. As it is, I'm going to live out this war as "mad old Friedrich", so that I can return again to Schleiden and become Butcher Friedrich that everyone knew and respected before all this mess began.'

As the weeks passed it became apparent that Friedrich took a particular liking to Topthorn. Knowing he had been ill he took more time and care over him, attending to the slightest sore before it could develop and make life uncomfortable for Topthorn. He was kind to me as well, but I think he never had the same affection for me. It was noticeable that he would often stand back and simply gaze at Topthorn with love and glowing admiration in his eyes. There seemed to be an empathy between them, that of one old soldier to another.

The summer passed slowly into autumn and it became clear that our time with Friedrich was coming to an end. Such was Friedrich's attachment to Topthorn by now that he volunteered to ride him out on the gun team exercises that were to precede the autumn campaign. Of course all the gunners laughed at the suggestion but they were always short of good horsemen – and no one denied he was that – and so we found ourselves the leading pair once again with mad old Friedrich riding up on Topthorn. We had found at last a true friend and one we could trust implicitly.

'If I have to die out here away from my home,' Friedrich confided in Topthorn one day, 'I would rather die alongside you. But I'll do my best to see to it that we all get through and get back home – that much I promise you.'

CHAPTER 14

SO FRIEDRICH RODE WITH US THAT AUTUMN DAY when we went to war again. The gun troop was resting at midday under the welcome shade of a large chestnut wood that covered both banks of a silver glinting river that was full of splashing, laughing men. As we moved in amongst the trees and the guns were unhitched, I saw that the entire wood was crowded with resting soldiers, their helmets, packs and rifles lying beside them. They sat back against the trees smoking, or lay out flat on their backs and slept.

As we had come to expect, a crowd of them soon came over to fondle the two golden Haflingers, but one young soldier approached Topthorn and stood looking up at him, his face full of open admiration. 'Now there's a horse,' he said, calling his friend over. 'Come and look at this one, Karl. Have you ever seen a finer looking animal? He has the head of an Arab. You can see the speed of an English thoroughbred in his legs and the strength of a Hanoverian in his back and in his neck. He has the best of everything,' and he reached up and gently rubbed his fist against Topthorn's nose.

'Don't you ever think about anything else except horses, Rudi?' said his companion, keeping his distance. 'Three years I've known you and not a day goes by without you going on about the wretched creatures. I know you were brought up with them on your farm, but I still can't understand what it is that you see in them. They are just four legs, a head and a tail, all controlled by a very little brain that can't think beyond food and drink.'

'How can you say that?' said Rudi. 'Just look at him, Karl. Can you not see that he's something special? This one isn't just any old horse. There's a nobility in his eye, a regal serenity about him. Does he not personify all that men try to be and never can be? I tell you, my friend, there's divinity in a horse, and specially in a horse like this. God got it right the day he created them.

112

And to find a horse like this in the middle of this filthy abomination of a war, is for me like finding a butterfly on a dung heap. We don't belong in the same universe as a creature like this.'

To me the soldiers had appeared to become younger as the war went on, and certainly Rudi was no exception to this. Under his short cropped hair that was still damp from wearing his helmet, he looked barely the same age as my Albert as I remembered him. And like so many of them now he looked, without his helmet, like a child dressed up as a soldier.

When Friedrich led us down to the river to drink, Rudi and his friend came with us. Topthorn lowered his head into the water beside me and shook it vigorously as he usually did, showering me all over my face and neck, and bringing me sweet relief from the heat. He drank long and deep and afterwards we stood together for a few moments on the river bank watching the soldiers frolicking in the water. The hill back up into the woods was steep and rutty, so it was no surprise that Topthorn stumbled once or twice – he had never been as surefooted as I was – but he regained his balance each time and plodded on beside me up the hill. However I did notice that he was moving rather wearily and sluggishly, that each step as we went up was becoming more and more of an effort for him. His breathing was suddenly short and rasping. Then, as we neared the shade of the trees Topthorn stumbled to his knees and did not get up again. I stopped for a moment to give him time to get up, but he did not. He lay where he was, breathing heavily and lifted his head once to look at me. It was an appeal for help – I could see it in his eyes. Then he slumped forward on his face, rolled over and was quite still. His tongue hung from his mouth and his eyes looked up at me without seeing me. I bent down to nuzzle him, pushing at his neck in a frantic effort to make him move, to make him wake up; but I knew instinctively that he was already dead, that I had lost my best and dearest friend. Friedrich was down on his knees beside him, his ear pressed to Topthorn's chest. He shook his head as he sat back and looked up at the group of men that had by now gathered around us. 'He's dead,' Friedrich said quietly, and then more angrily, 'For God's sake, he's dead.' His face was heavy with sadness. 'Why?' he said, 'Why does this war have to destroy anything and everything that's fine and beautiful?' He covered his eyes with his hands and Rudi lifted him gently to his feet.

'Nothing you can do, old man,' he said. 'He's well out of it. Come on.' But old Friedrich would not be led away. I turned once more to Topthorn, still licking and nuzzling him where he lay, although I knew and indeed understood by now the finality of death, but in my grief I felt only that I wanted to stay with him to comfort him.

The veterinary officer attached to the troop came running down the hill followed by all the officers and men in the troop who had just heard what had happened. After a brief inspection he too pronounced Topthorn to be dead. 'I thought so. I told you so,' he said almost to himself. 'They can't do it. I see it all the time. Too much work on short rations and living out all winter. I see it all the time. A horse like this can only stand so much. Heart failure, poor fellow. It makes me angry every time it happens. We should not treat horses like this – we treat our machines better.'

'He was a friend,' said Friedrich simply, kneeling down again over Topthorn and removing his head-collar. The soldiers stood all around us in complete silence looking down at the prostrate form of Topthorn, in a moment of spontaneous respect and sadness. Perhaps it was because they had known him for a long time and he had in some way become part of their lives.

As we stood silent on the hillside I heard the first whistle of a shell above us and saw the first explosion as the shell landed in the river. Suddenly the wood was alive with shouting, rushing soldiers and the shells were falling around us everywhere. The men in the river, half-naked and screaming, ran up into the trees and the shelling seemed to follow them. Trees crashed to the ground and horses and men came running out of the wood in the direction of the ridge above us.

My first inclination was to run with them, to run anywhere to escape the shelling; but Topthorn lay dead at my feet and I would not abandon him. Friedrich who was holding me now tried all he could to drag me away up behind the shoulder of the hill, shouting and screaming at me to come if I wanted to live; but no man can move a horse that does not wish to be moved, and I did not want to go. As the shelling intensified and he found himself more and more isolated from his friends as they swarmed away up the hill and out of sight, he threw down my reins and tried to make his escape. But he was too slow and he had left it too late. He never reached the woods. He was struck down only a few paces from Topthorn, rolled back down the hill and lay still beside him. The last I saw of my troop were the bobbing white manes of the two little Haflingers as they struggled to pull the gun up through the trees with the gunners hauling frantically on their reins and straining to push the gun from behind.

CHAPTER 15

I STOOD BY TOPTHORN AND FRIEDRICH ALL THAT day and into the night, leaving them only once to drink briefly at the river. The shelling moved back and forth along the valley, showering grass and earth and trees into the air and leaving behind great craters that smoked as if the earth itself was on fire. But any fear I might have had was overwhelmed by a powerful sense of sadness and love that compelled me to stay with Topthorn for as long as I could. I knew that once I left him I would be alone in the world again, that I would no longer have his strength and support beside me. So I stayed with him and waited.

I remember it was near first light and I was cropping

the grass close to where they lay when I heard through the crump and whistle of the shells the whining sound of motors accompanied by a terrifying rattle of steel that set my ears back against my head. It came from over the ridge from the direction in which the soldiers had disappeared, a grating, roaring sound that came ever nearer by the minute; and louder again as the shelling died away completely.

Although at the time I did not know it as such, the first tank I ever saw came over the rise of the hill with the cold light of dawn behind it, a great grey lumbering monster that belched out smoke from behind as it rocked down the hillside towards me. I hesitated only for a few moments before blind terror tore me at last from Topthorn's side and sent me bolting down the hill towards the river. I crashed into the river without even knowing whether I should find my feet or not and was half-way up the wooded hill on the other side before I dared stop and turn to see if it was still chasing me. I should never have looked, for the one monster had become several monsters and they were rolling inexorably down towards me, already past the place where Topthorn lay with Friedrich on the shattered hillside. I waited, secure, I thought, in the shelter of the trees and watched the tanks ford the river before turning once more to run.

I ran I knew not where. I ran till I could no longer hear that dreadful rattle and until the guns seemed far away. I remember crossing a river again, galloping through empty farmyards, jumping fences and ditches and abandoned trenches, and clattering through deserted, ruined villages before I found myself grazing that evening in a lush, wet meadow and drinking from a clear, pebbly brook. And then exhaustion finally overtook me, sapped the strength from my legs and forced me to lie down and sleep.

When I woke it was dark and the guns were firing once more all around me. No matter where I looked it seemed, the sky was lit with the yellow flashes of gun-fire and intermittent white glowing lights that pained my eyes and showered daylight briefly on to the country-side around me. Whichever way I went it seemed it had to be towards the guns. Better therefore I thought to stay where I was. Here at least I had grass in plenty and water to drink.

I had made up my mind to do just that when there was an explosion of white light above my head and the rattle of a machine-gun split the night air, the bullets whipping into the ground beside me. I ran again and kept running into the night, stumbling frequently in the ditches and hedges until the fields lost their grass and the trees were mere stumps against the flashing skyline. Wherever I went now there were great craters in the ground filled with murky, stagnant water.

It was as I staggered out of one such crater that I lumbered into an invisible coil of barbed wire that first snagged and then trapped my foreleg. As I kicked out wildly to free myself, I felt the barbs tearing into my foreleg before I broke clear. From then on I could manage only to limp on slowly into the night, feeling my way forward. Even so I must have walked for miles, but where to and where from I shall never know. All the while my leg pulsated with pain and on every side of me the great guns were sounding out and rifle-fire spat into the night. Bleeding, bruised and terrified beyond belief, I longed only to be with Topthorn again. He would know which way to go, I told myself. He would know.

I stumbled on into the night guided only by the belief that where the night was at its blackest there alone I might find some safety from the shelling. Behind me the thunder and lightning of the bombardment was so terrible in its intensity, turning the deep black of night into unnatural day, that I could not contemplate going back even though I knew that it was in the direction that Topthorn lay. There was some gunfire ahead of me and on both sides of me, but I could see away in the distance a black horizon of undisturbed night and so moved on steadily towards it.

My wounded leg was stiffening up all the time in the cold of the night and it pained me now even to lift it. Very soon I found I could put no weight on it at all. This was to be the longest night of my life, a nightmare of agony, terror and loneliness. I suppose it was only a strong instinct to survive that compelled me to walk on and kept me on my feet. I sensed that my only chance lay in putting the noise of the battle as far behind me as possible, so I had to keep moving. From time to time rifle fire and machine-gun fire would crackle all around me, and I would stand paralysed with fear, terrified to move in any direction until the firing stopped and I found my muscles could move once more.

To begin with I found the mists hovering only in the depths of the craters I passed, but after some hours I found myself increasingly surrounded in a thick, smoky, autumnal mist through which I could see only the vague shades and shapes of dark and light around me. Almost blinded now I relied totally on the ever more distant roar and rumble of the bombardment, keeping it all the time behind me and moving towards the darker more silent world ahead of me.

Dawn was already brightening the gloom of the mist when I heard the sound of hushed, urgent voices ahead of me. I stood quite still and listened, straining my eyes to find the people to whom they belonged. 'Stand to, get a move on. Get a move on lads.' The voices were muffled in the mist. There was a sound of rushing feet and clattering rifles. 'Pick it up, lad, pick it up. What do you think you're about? Now clean that rifle off and do it sharpish.' A long silence followed and I moved gingerly towards the voices, both tempted and terrified at the same time.

'There it is again, Sarge. I saw something, honest I did.'

'What was it then, son? The whole German ruddy army, or just one or two of them out for a morning stroll?'

'Weren't a man, Sarge, nor even a German neither – looked more like an 'orse or cow to me.'

'A cow or a horse? Out there in no man's land? And how the blazes d'you think it got there? Son, you've been staying up too late – your eyes is playing tricks on you.'

'I 'eard it too, Sarge, an all. Honest Sarge, cross me 'eart.'

'Well, I can't see nothing, I can't see nothing, son, and that's 'cos there's nothing there. You're all of a jitter son, and your jittering has brought the whole ruddy battalion on stand-to half an hour early, and who's going to be a popular little lad when I tells the lieutenant all about it? Spoiled his beauty sleep, haven't you, son? You gorn and woken up all them lovely captains and majors and brigadiers, and all them nice sergeants an all, just 'cos you thought you seen a flaming horse.' And then in a louder voice that was intended to carry further. 'But seeing as how we're all stood to and there's a pea-soup flaming London smog out there, and seeing as how Jerry likes to come a-knocking on our little dugouts just when we can't see him a-coming, I wants you lads to keep your eyes peeled back and wide open – then we'll all live to eat our breakfasts, if it's on this morning. There'll be a rum ration coming round in a few minutes – that'll light you up – but until then I want every one of your eyes skinned.'

As he spoke I limped away. I could feel myself shaking from head to tail in dreadful anticipation of the next bullet or shell, and I wanted only to be alone, away from any noise whatever, whether or not it appeared to be threatening. In my weakened, frightened condition any sense of reason had left me and I wandered now through the mists until my good legs could drag me no further. I stood at last, resting my bleeding leg, on a soft, fresh mound of mud beside a foul-smelling, water-filled crater, and I snuffled the ground in vain for something to eat. But the earth where I stood was bare of grass and I had neither the energy nor the will at that moment to move another step forward. I lifted my head again to look about me in case I should discover any grass nearby and as I did so I felt the first sunlight filter in through the mist and touch my back sending gentle shivers of warmth through my cold, cramped body.

Within minutes the mist began to clear away and I saw for the first time that I stood in a wide corridor of mud, a wasted, shattered landscape, between two vast unending rolls of barbed wire that stretched away into the distance behind me and in front of me. I remembered I had been in such a place once before, that day when I had charged across it with Topthorn beside me. This was what the soldiers called 'no man's land'.

CHAPTER 16

FROM BOTH SIDES OF ME I HEARD A GRADUAL crescendo of excitement and laughter rippling along the trenches, interspersed with barked orders that everyone was to keep their heads down and no one was to shoot. From my vantage point on the mound I could see only an occasional glimpse of a steel helmet, my only evidence that the voices I was hearing did indeed belong to real people. There was the sweet smell of cooking food wafting towards me and I lifted my nose to savour it. It was sweeter than the sweetest bran-mash I had ever tasted and it had a tinge of salt about it. I was drawn first one way and then the other by this promise of warm food, but each time I neared the trenches on either side I met an impenetrable barrier of loosely coiled barbed wire. The soldiers cheered me on as I came closer, showing their heads fully now over the trenches and beckoning me towards them; and when I had to turn back at the wire and crossed no man's land to the other side, I was welcomed again there by a chorus of whistling and clapping, but again I could find no way through the wire. I must have criss-crossed no man's land for much of that morning, and found at long last in the middle of this blasted wilderness a small patch of coarse, dank grass growing on the lip of an old crater.

I was busying myself at tearing the last of this away when I saw, out of the corner of my eye, a man in a grey uniform clamber up out of the trenches, waving a white flag above his head. I looked up as he began to clip his way methodically through the wire and then pull it aside. All this time there was much argument and noisy consternation from the other side; and soon a small, helmeted figure in a flapping khaki greatcoat climbed up into no man's land. He too held up a white handkerchief in one hand and began also to work his way through the wire towards me.

The German was through the wire first, leaving a

narrow gap behind him. He approached me slowly across no man's land, calling out to me all the while to come towards him. He reminded me at once of dear old Friedrich for he was, like Friedrich, a grey-haired man in an untidy, unbuttoned uniform and he spoke gently to me. In one hand he held a rope; the other hand he stretched out towards me. He was still far too far away for me to see clearly, but an offered hand in my experience was often cupped and there was enough promise in that for me to limp cautiously towards him. On both sides the trenches were lined now with cheering men, standing on the parapets waving their helmets above their heads.

'Oi, boyo!' The shout came from behind me and was urgent enough to stop me. I turned to see the small man in khaki weaving and jinking his way across no man's land, one hand held high above his head carrying the white handkerchief. 'Oi, boyo! Where you going? Hang on a bit. You're going the wrong way, see.'

The two men who were coming towards me could not have been more different. The one in grey was the taller of the two and as he came nearer I could see his face was lined and creased with years. Everything about him was slow and gentle under his ill-fitting uniform. He wore no helmet, but instead the peakless cap with the red band I knew so well sitting carelessly on the back of his head. The little man in khaki reached us, out of breath, his face red and still smooth with youth, his round helmet with the broad rim fallen askew over one ear. For a few strained, silent moments the two stood yards apart from each other, eyeing one another warily and saying not a word. It was the young man in khaki who broke the silence and spoke first.

'Now what do we do?' he said, walking towards us and looking at the German who stood head and shoulders above him. 'There's two of us here and one horse to split between us. 'Course, King Solomon had the answer, didn't he now? But it's not very practical in this case is it? And what's worse, I can't speak a word of German, and I can see you can't understand what the hell I'm talking about, can you? Oh hell, I should never have come out here, I knew I shouldn't. Can't think what came over me, and all for a muddy old horse too.'

'But I can, I can speak a little bad English,' said the older man, still holding out his cupped hand under my nose. It was full of black bread broken into pieces, a tit-bit I was familiar enough with but usually found too bitter for my taste. However I was now too hungry to be choosy and as he was speaking I soon emptied his hand. 'I speak only a little English – like a schoolboy – but it's enough I think for us.' And even as he spoke I felt a rope slip slowly around my neck and tighten. 'As for our other problem, since I have been here the first, then the horse is mine. Fair, no? Like your cricket?'

'Cricket! Cricket!' said the young man. 'Who's ever heard of that barbarous game in Wales? That's a game for the rotten English. Rugby, that's my game, and that's not a game. That's a religion that is – where I come from. I played scrum-half for Maesteg before the war stopped me, and at Maesteg we say that a loose ball is our ball.'

'Sorry?' said the German, his eyebrows furrowed with concern. 'I cannot understand what you mean by this.'

'Doesn't matter, Jerry. Not important, not any more. We could have settled all this peaceful like, Jerry – the the war I mean – and I'd be back in my valley and you'd be back in yours. Still, not your fault I don't suppose. Nor mine, neither come to that.'

By now the cheering from both sides had subsided and both armies looked on in total silence as the two men talked together beside me. The Welshman was stroking my nose and feeling my ears. 'You know horses then?' said the tall German. 'How bad is his wounded leg? Is it broken do you think? He seems not to walk on it.'

The Welshman bent over and lifted my leg gently and expertly, wiping away the mud from around the wound. 'He's in a mess right enough, but I don't think it's broken, Jerry. It's a bad wound though, a deep gash – wire by the look of it. Got to get him seen to quick else the poison will set in and then there won't be a lot anyone could do for him. Cut like that, he must have lost a lot of blood already. Question is though, who takes him? We've got a veterinary hospital somewhere back behind our lines that could take care of him, but I expect you've got one too.'

'Yes, I think so. Somewhere it must be, but I do not know exactly where,' the German said slowly. And then he dug deep in his pocket and produced a coin. 'You choose the side you want, "head or tail", I think you say. I will show the coin to everyone on both sides and everyone will know that whichever side wins the horse it is only by chance. Then no one loses any pride, yes? And everyone will be happy.'

The Welshman looked up admiringly and smiled. 'All right then, you go ahead, Jerry, you show them the coin and then you toss and I'll call.'

The German held the coin up in the sun and then turned a full slow circle before spinning it high and glinting into the air. As it fell to the ground the Welshman called out in a loud, resonant voice so that all the world could hear, 'Heads!'

'Well,' said the German stooping to pick it up. 'That's the face of my Kaiser looking up at me out of the mud, and he does not look pleased with me. So I am afraid you have won. The horse is yours. Take good care of him, my friend,' and he picked up the rope again and handed it to the Welshman. As he did so he held out his other hand in a gesture of friendship and reconciliation, a smile lighting his worn face. 'In an hour, maybe, or two,' he said. 'We will be trying our best again each other to kill. God only knows why we do it, and I think he has maybe forgotten why. Goodbye Welshman. We have shown them, haven't we? We have shown them that any problem can be solved between people if only they can trust each other. That is all it needs, no?'

The little Welshman shook his head in disbelief as he

took the rope. 'Jerry, boyo, I think if they would let you and me have an hour or two out here together, we could sort out this whole wretched mess. There would be no more weeping widows and crying children in my valley and no more in yours. If the worse came to the worst we could decide it all on the flip of a coin, couldn't we now?'

'If we did,' said the German with a chuckle. 'If we did it that way, then it would be our turn to win. And maybe your Lloyd George would not like that.' And he put his hands on the Welshman's shoulders for a moment. 'Take care, my friend, and good luck. Auf Wiedersehen.' And he turned away and walked slowly back across no man's land to the wire.

'Same to you, boyo,' the Welshman shouted after him, and then he too turned and led me away back towards the line of khaki soldiers who began now to laugh and cheer with delight as I limped towards them through the gap in the wire.

CHAPTER 17

IT WAS ONLY WITH THE GREATEST DIFFICULTY THAT I stayed standing on my three good legs in the veterinary wagon that carried me that morning away from the heroic little Welshman who had brought me in. A milling crowd of soldiers surrounded me to cheer me on my way. But out on the long rattling roads I was very soon shaken off my balance and fell in an ungainly, uncomfortable heap on the floor of the wagon. My injured leg throbbed terribly as the wagon rocked from side to side on its slow journey away from the battle front. The wagon was drawn by two stocky black horses, both well groomed out and immaculate in well-oiled harness. Weakened by long hours of pain and starvation I had not the strength even to get to my feet when I felt the wheels below me running at last on smooth cobblestones and the wagon came to a jerking standstill in the warm, pale autumn sunshine. My arrival was greeted by a chorus of excited neighing and I raised my head to look. I could just see over the sideboards a wide, cobbled courtyard with magnificent stables on either side and a great house with turrets beyond. Over every stable-door were the heads of inquisitive horses, ears pricked. There were men in khaki walking everywhere, and a few were running now towards me, one of them carrying a rope halter.

Unloading was painful, for I had little strength left and my legs had gone numb after the long journey. But they got me to my feet and walked me backwards gently down the ramp. I found myself the centre of anxious and admiring attention in the middle of the courtyard, surrounded by a cluster of soldiers who inspected minutely every part of me, feeling me all over.

'What in thunder do you think you're about, you lot?' came a booming voice echoing across the court-yard. 'It's an 'orse. It's an 'orse just like the others.' A huge man was striding towards us, his boots crisp on the cobbles. His heavy red face was half hidden by the shade of his peaked cap that almost touched his nose and by a ginger moustache that spread upwards from his lips to his ears. 'It may be a famous 'orse. It may be the only thundering 'orse in the 'ole thundering war brought in alive from no man's land. But it is only an 'orse and a dirty 'orse at that. I've had some rough looking specimens brought in here in my time, but this is the scruffiest, dirtiest, muddiest 'orse I have ever seen. He's a thundering disgrace and you're all stood about looking at him.' He wore three broad stripes on his arm and the creases in his immaculate khaki uniform were razor sharp. 'Now there's a hundred or more sick 'orses 'ere in this 'ospital and there's just twelve of us to look after them. This 'ere young layabout was detailed to look after this one when he arrived, so the rest of you blighters can get back to your duties. Move it, you idle monkeys, move it!' And the men scattered in all directions, leaving me with a young soldier who began to lead me away towards a stable. 'And you,' came that booming voice again. 'Major Martin will be down from the 'ouse in ten minutes to examine that 'orse. Make sure that 'orse is so thundering clean and thundering shiny so's you could use him as a shaving mirror, right?'

'Yes, Sergeant,' came the reply. A reply that sent a sudden shiver of recognition through me. Quite where I had heard the voice before I did now know. I knew only that those two words sent a tremor of joy and hope and expectation through my body and warmed me from the inside out. He led me slowly across the cobbles, and I tried all the while to see his face better. But he kept just that much ahead of me so that all I could see was a neatly shaven neck and a pair of pink ears.

'How the divil did you get yourself stuck out there in no man's land, you old silly?' he said. 'That's what everyone wants to know ever since the message came back that they'd be bringing you in here. And how the divil did you get yourself in such a state? I swear there's not an inch of you that isn't covered in mud or blood. Job to tell what you look like under all that mess. Still, we'll soon see. I'll tie you up here and get the worst of it off in the open air. Then I'll brush you up in the proper manner afore the officer gets here. Come on, you silly you. Once I've got you cleaned up then the officer can see you and he'll tidy up the nasty cut of yours. Can't give you food, I'm sorry to say, nor any water, not till he says so. That's what the sergeant told me. That's just in case they have to operate on you.' And the way he whistled as he cleaned out the brushes was the whistle that went with the voice I knew. It confirmed my rising hopes and I knew then that I could not be mistaken. In my overwhelming delight I reared up on my back legs and cried out to him to recognise me. I wanted to make him see who I was. 'Hey, careful there, you silly. Nearly had my hat off,' he said gently, keeping a firm hold on the rope and smoothing my nose as he always had done whenever I was unhappy. 'No need for that. You'll be all right. Lot of fuss about nothing. Knew a young horse once just like you, proper jumpy he was till I got to know him and he got to know me.'

'You talking to them horses again, Albert?' came a voice from inside the next stable. 'Gawd's strewth! What makes you think they understand a perishing word you say?'

'Some of them may not, David,' said Albert. 'But one day, one day one of them will. He'll come in here and he'll recognise my voice. He's bound to come in here. And then you'll see a horse that understands every word that's said to him.'

'You're not on about your Joey again?' The head

that came with the voice leant over the stable-door. 'Won't you never give it up, Berty? I've told you before if I've told you a thousand times. They say there's near half a million ruddy horses out here and you joined the Veterinary Corps just on the off-chance you might come across him.' I pawed the ground with my bad leg in an effort to make Albert look at me more closely, but he just patted my neck and set to work cleaning me up. 'There's just one chance in half a million that your Joey walks in here. You got to be more realistic. He could be dead – a lot of them are. He could have gorn orf to ruddy Palestine with the Yeomanry. He could be any-where along hundreds of miles of trenches. If you weren't so ruddy good with horses, and if you weren't the best friend I had, I'd think you'd gorn and gorn a bit screwy the way you go on about your Joey.'

'You'll understand why when you see him, David,' Albert said crouching down to scrape the caked mud off my underside. 'You'll see. There's no horse like him anywhere in the whole world. He's a bright red bay with a black mane and tail. He has a white cross on his forehead and four white socks that are all even to the last inch. He stands over sixteen hands and he's perfect from head to tail. I can tell you, I can tell you that when you see him you'll know him. I could pick him out of a crowd of a thousand horses. There's just something about him. Captain Nicholls, you know, him that's dead now, the one I told you about that bought Joey from my father, him that sent me Joey's picture; he knew it. He saw it the first time he set eyes on him. I'll find him, David. That's what I came all this way for and I'm going to find him. Either I'll find him, or he'll find me. I told you, I made him a promise and I'm going to keep it.'

'You're round the ruddy twist, Berty,' said his friend opening a stable-door and coming over to examine my leg. 'Round the ruddy twist, that's all I can say.' He picked up my hoof and lifted it gently. 'This one's got a white sock on his front legs anyway – that's as far as I can tell under all this blood and mud. I'll just sponge the wound away a bit, clean it up for you whilst I'm here. You'll never get this one cleaned up in time else. And I've finished mucking out my ruddy stables. Not a lot else to do and it looks as if you could do with a hand. Old Sergeant Thunder won't mind, not if I've done all he told me, and I have.'

The two men worked tirelessly on me, scraping and brushing and washing. I stood quite still trying only to nuzzle Albert to make him turn and look at me. But he was busying at my tail and my hindquarters now.

'Three,' said his friend, washing off another of my hooves. 'That's three white socks.'

'Turn it up, David,' said Albert. 'I know what you think. I know everyone thinks I'll never find him. There's thousands of army horses with four white socks – I know that, but there's only one with a blaze in the shape of a cross on the forehead. And how many horses shine red like fire in the evening sun? I tell you there's not another one like him, not in the whole wide world.'

'Four,' said David. 'That's four legs and four white socks. Only the cross on the fore'ead now, and a splash of red paint on this muddy mess of a horse and you'll have your Joey standing 'ere.'

'Don't tease,' said Albert quietly. 'Don't tease, David. You know how serious I am about Joey. It'll mean all the world to me to find him again. Only friend I ever had afore I came to the war. I told you. I grew up with him, I did. Only creature on this earth I felt any kinship for.'

David was standing now by my head. He lifted my mane and brushed gently at first then vigorously at my forehead, blowing the dust away from my eyes. He peered closely and then set to again brushing down towards the end of my nose and up again between my ears till I tossed my head with impatience.

'Berty,' he said quietly. 'I'm not teasing, honest I'm not. Not now. You said your Joey had four white socks, all even to the inch? Right?'

'Right,' said Albert, still brushing away at my tail.

'And you said Joey had a white cross on his forehead?'

'Right,' Albert was still completely disinterested.

'Now I have never ever seen a horse like that, Berty,' said David, using his hand to smooth down the hair on my forehead. 'Wouldn't have thought it possible.'

'Well, it is, I tell you,' said Albert sharply. 'And he was red, flaming red in the sunlight, like I said.'

'I wouldn't have thought it possible,' his friend went on, keeping his voice in check. 'Not until now that is.'

'Oh, pack it in, David,' Albert said, and there was a genuine irritation in his voice now. 'I've told you, haven't I? I told you I'm serious about Joey.'

'So am I, Berty. Dead serious. No messing, I'm serious. This horse has four white socks – all evenly marked like you said. This horse has a clear white cross on his head.

This horse, as you can see for yourself, has a black mane and tail. This horse stands over sixteen hands and when he's cleaned up he'll look pretty as a picture. And this horse is a red bay under all that mud, just like you said, Berty.'

As David was speaking Albert suddenly dropped my tail and moved slowly around me running his hand along my back. Then at last we stood facing one another. There was a rougher hue to his face I thought; he had more lines around his eyes and he was a broader, bigger man in his uniform than I remembered him. But he was my Albert, and there was no doubt about it, he was my Albert.

'Joey?' he said tentatively, looking into my eyes. 'Joey?' I tossed up my head and called out to him in my happiness, so that the sound echoed around the yard and brought horses and men to the door of their stables. 'It could be,' said Albert quietly. 'You're right David, it could be him. It sounds like him even. But there's one way I know to be sure,' and he untied my rope and pulled the halter off my head. Then he turned and walked away to the gateway before facing me, cupping his hands to his lips and whistling. It was his owl whistle, the same low, stuttering whistle he had used to call me when we were walking out together back at home on the farm all those long years before. Suddenly there was no longer any pain in my leg, and I trotted easily over towards him and buried my nose in his shoulder. 'It's him, David,' Albert said, putting his arms around my neck and hanging on to my mane. 'It's my Joey. I've found him. He's come back to me just like I said he would.'

'See?' said David wryly. 'What did I tell you? See? Not often wrong, am I?'

'Not often,' Albert said. 'Not often, and not this time.'

CHAPTER 18

IN THE EUPHORIC DAYS THAT FOLLOWED OUR reunion, the nightmare I had lived through seemed to fade into unreality, and the war itself was suddenly a million miles away and of no consequence. At last there were no guns to be heard, and the only vivid reminder that suffering and conflict was still going on were the regular arrivals of the veterinary wagons from the front.

Major Martin cleaned my wound and stitched it up; and though at first I could still put little weight on it, I felt in myself stronger with every day that passed. Albert was with me again, and that in itself was medicine enough; but properly fed once more with warm mash each morning and a never ending supply of sweet-scented hay, my recovery seemed only a matter of time. Albert, like the other veterinary orderlies, had many other horses to care for, but he would spend every spare minute he could find fussing over me in the stable. To the other soldiers I was something of a celebrity, so I was scarcely ever left alone in my stable. There always seemed to be one or two faces looking admiringly over my door. Even old Thunder, as they called the sergeant, would inspect me over zealously, and when the others were not about he would fondle my ears and tickle me under my throat saying, 'Quite a boy, aren't you? Thundering fine horse if ever I saw one. You get better now, d'you hear?'

But time passed and I did not get better. One morning I found myself quite unable to finish my mash and every sharp sound, like the kick of a bucket or the rattle of the bolt on the stable door, seemed to set me on edge and made me suddenly tense from head to tail. My forelegs in particular would not work as they should. They were stiff and tired, and I felt a great weight of pain all along my spine, creeping into my neck and even my face.

Albert noticed something was wrong when he saw

the mash I had left in my bucket. 'What's the matter with you, Joey?' he said anxiously, and he reached out his hand to stroke me in the way he often did when he was concerned. Even the sight of his hand coming towards me, normally a welcome sign of affection, struck an alarm in me, and I backed away from him into the corner of the stable. As I did so I found that the stiffness in my front legs would hardly allow me to move. I stumbled backwards, falling against the brick wall at the back of the stable, and leaning there heavily. 'I thought something was wrong yesterday,' said Albert, standing still now in the middle of the stable. 'Thought you were a bit off colour then. Your back's as stiff as a board and you're covered in sweat. What the divil have you been up to, you old silly?' He moved slowly now towards me and although his touch still sent an irrational tremor of fear through me, I stood my ground and allowed him to stroke me. 'P'raps it was something you picked up on your travels. P'raps you ate something poisonous, is that it? But then that would have shown itself before now, surely? You'll be fine, Joey, but I'll go and fetch Major Martin just in case. He'll look you over and if there's anything wrong put you right "quick as a twick", as my father used to say. Wonder what he would think now if he could see us together? He never believed I'd find you either, said I was a fool to go. Said it was a fool's errand and that I'd likely get myself killed in the process. But he was a different man, Joey, after you left. He knew he'd done wrong, and that seemed to take all the nastiness out of him. He seemed to live only to make up for what he'd done. He stopped his Tuesday drinking sessions, looked after Mother as he used to do when I was little, and he even began to treat me right – didn't treat me like a workhorse any more.'

I knew from the soft tone of his voice that he was trying to calm me, as he had done all those long years ago when I was a wild and frightened colt. Then his words had soothed me, but now I could not stop myself from trembling. Every nerve in my body seemed to be taut and I was breathing heavily. Every fibre of me was consumed by a totally inexplicable sense of fear and dread. 'I'll be back in a minute, Joey,' he said. 'Don't you worry. You'll be all right. Major Martin will fix you – he's a miracle with horses is that man.' And he backed away from me and went out.

It was not long before he was back again with his friend, David, with Major Martin and Sergeant

Thunder; but only Major Martin came inside the stable to examine me. The others leaned over the stable-door and watched. He approached me cautiously, crouching down by my foreleg to examine my wound. Then he ran his hands all over me from my ears, down my back to my tail, before standing back to survey me from the other side of the stable. He was shaking his head ruefully as he turned to speak to the others.

'What do you think, Sergeant?' he asked.

'Same as you, from the look of 'im, sir,' said Sergeant Thunder. ''E's standing there like a block of wood; tail stuck out, can't 'ardly move his head. Not much doubt about it, is there sir?'

'None,' said Major Martin. 'None whatsoever. We've had a lot of it out here. If it isn't confounded rusty barbed wire, then it's shrapnel wounds. One little fragment left inside, one cut – that's all it takes. I've seen it time and again. I'm sorry my lad,' the major said, putting his hand on Albert's shoulder to console him. 'I know how much this horse means to you. But there's precious little we can do for him, not in his condition.'

'What do you mean, sir?' Albert asked, a tremor in his voice. 'How do you mean, sir? What's the matter with him, sir? Can't be a lot wrong, can there? He was right as rain yesterday, 'cept he wasn't finishing his feed. Little stiff p'raps but otherwise right as rain he was.'

'It's tetanus, son,' said Sergeant Thunder. 'Lock-jaw they calls it. It's written all over 'im. That wound of 'is must have festered afore we got 'im 'ere. And once an 'orse 'as tetanus there's very little chance, very little indeed.'

'Best to end it quickly,' Major Martin said. 'No point in an animal suffering. Better for him, and better for you.'

'No, sir,' Albert protested, still incredulous. 'No you can't, sir. Not with Joey. We must try something. There must be something you can do. You can't just give up, sir. You can't. Not with Joey.'

David spoke up now in support. 'Begging your pardon, sir,' he said. 'But I remembers you telling us when we first come here that a horse's life is p'raps even more important than a man's, 'cos an horse hasn't got no evil in him 'cepting any that's put there by men. I remembers you saying that our job in the veterinary corps was to work night and day, twenty-six hours a day if need be to save and help every horse that we could, that every horse was valuable in hisself and valuable to the war effort. No horse, no guns. No horse, no ammunition. No horse, no cavalry. No horse, no ambulances. No horse, no water for the troops at the front. Lifeline of the whole army, you said, sir. We must never give up, you said, 'cos where there's life there's still hope. That's all what you said, sir, begging your pardon, sir.'

'You watch your lip, son,' said Sergeant Thunder sharply. 'That's no way to speak to an officer. If the major 'ere thought there was a chance in a million of savin' this poor animal, 'e'd have a crack at it, wouldn't you sir? Isn't that right, sir?'

Major Martin looked hard at Sergeant Thunder, taking his meaning, and then nodded slowly. 'All right, Sergeant. You made your point. Of course there's a chance,' he said carefully. 'But if once we start with a case of tetanus, then it's a full-time job for one man for a month or more, and even then the horse has hardly more than one chance in a thousand, if that.'

'Please sir,' Albert pleaded. 'Please sir. I'll do it all, sir, and I'll fit in my other horses too, sir. Honest I would, sir.'

'And I'll help him, sir,' David said. 'All the lads will. I know they will. You see sir, that Joey's a bit special for everyone here, what with his being Berty's own horse back home an all.'

'That's the spirit, son,' said Sergeant Thunder. 'And it's true, sir, there is something a bit special about this one, you know, after all he's been through. With your permission sir, I think we ought to give 'im that chance. You 'ave my personal guarantee sir that no other 'orse will be neglected. Stables will be run shipshape and Bristol fashion, like always.'

Major Martin put his hands on the stable door. 'Right, Sergeant,' he said. 'You're on. I like a challenge as well as the next man. I want a sling rigged up in here. This horse must not be allowed to get off his legs. Once he's down he'll never get up again. I want a note added to standing orders, Sergeant, that no one's to talk in anything but a whisper in this yard. He won't like any noise, not with tetanus. I want a bed of short, clean straw – and fresh every day. I want the windows covered over so that he's kept always in the dark. He's not to be fed any hay – he could choke on it – just milk and oatmeal gruel. And it's going to get worse before it gets better – if it does. You'll find his mouth will lock tighter as the days go by, but he must go on feeding and he must drink. If he doesn't then he'll die. I want a twenty-four-hour watch on this horse – that means a man posted in here all day and every day. Clear?'

'Yes, sir,' said Sergeant Thunder, smiling broadly under his moustache. 'And if I may say so, sir, I think you've made a very wise decision. I'll see to it, sir. Now, look lively you two layabouts. You heard what the officer said.'

That same day a sling was strung up around me and my weight supported from the beams above. Major Martin opened up my wound again, cleaned and cauterized it. He returned every few hours after that to examine me. It was Albert of course who stayed with me most of the time, holding up the bucket to my mouth so that I could suck in the warm milk or gruel. At nights David and he slept side by side in the corner of the stable, taking turns to watch me.

As I had come to expect, and as I needed, Albert talked to me all he could to comfort me, until sheer fatigue drove him back into his corner to sleep. He talked much of his father and mother and about the farm. He talked of a girl he had been seeing up in the village for the few months before he left for France. She didn't know anything about horses, he said, but that was her only fault.

The days passed slowly and painfully for me. The stiffness in my front legs spread to my back and intensified; my appetite was becoming more limited each day and I could scarcely summon the energy or enthusiasm to suck in the food I knew I needed to stay alive. In the darkest days of my illness, when I felt sure each day might be my last, only Alberts constant presence kept alive in me the will to live. His devotion, his unwavering faith that I would indeed recover, gave me the heart to go on. All around me I had friends, David and all the veterinary orderlies, Sergeant Thunder and Major Martin – they were all a source of great encouragement to me. I knew how desperately they were willing me to live; although I often wondered whether they wanted it for me or for Albert for I knew they held him in such high esteem. But on reflection I think perhaps they cared for both of us as if we were their brothers.

Then one winter's night after long painful weeks in the sling, I felt a sudden looseness in my throat and neck, so much so that I could call out, albeit softly for the first time. Albert was sitting in the corner of the stable as usual with his back against the wall, his knees drawn up and his elbows resting on his knees. His eyes were closed, so I nickered again softly, but it was loud enough to wake him. 'Was that you, Joey?' he asked, pulling himself to his feet. 'Was that you, you old silly? Do it again, Joey. I might have been dreaming. Do it again.' So I did and in so doing I lifted my head for the first time in weeks and shook it. David heard it too and was on his feet and shouting over the stable door for everyone to come. Within minutes the stable was full of excited soldiers. Sergeant Thunder pushed his way through and stood before me. 'Standing orders says whisper,' he said. 'And that was no thundering whisper I heard. What's up? What's all the 'ullabaloo?'

'He moved, Sarge,' Albert said. 'His head moved easily and he neighed.'

''Course 'e did, son,' said Sergeant Thunder. ''Course 'e did. 'E's going to make it. Like I said he would. I always told you 'e would, didn't I? And 'ave any of you layabouts ever known me to be wrong? Well, 'ave you?'

'Never, Sarge,' said Albert, grinning from ear to ear. 'He is getting better, isn't he Sarge? I'm not just imagining it, am I?'

'No, son,' said Sergeant Thunder. 'Your Joey is going to be all right by the looks of 'im, long as we keeps 'im quiet and so long as we don't rush 'im. I just 'opes that if I'm ever poorly I 'ave nurses around me that looks after me like you lot 'ave this 'orse. One thing, though, looking at you, I'd like them to be an 'ole lot prettier!'

Shortly after I found my legs again and then the stiffness left my back for ever. They took me out of the sling and walked me one spring morning out into the sunshine of the cobbled yard. It was a triumphant parade, with Albert leading me carefully walking backwards and talking to me all the while. 'You've done it, Joey. You've done it. Everyone says the war's going to be over quite soon – I know we've been saying that for a long time, but I feel it in my bones this time. It'll be finished before long and then we'll both be going home, back to the farm. I can't wait to see the look on Father's face when I bring you back up the lane. I just can't wait.'

CHAPTER 19

BUT THE WAR DID NOT END. INSTEAD IT SEEMED to move ever closer to us, and we heard once again the ominous rumble of gunfire. My convalescence was almost over now, and although still weak from my illness, I was already being used for light work around the veterinary hospital. I worked in a team of two, hauling hay and feed from the nearest station or pulling the dung cart around the yard. I felt fresh and eager for work once more. My legs and shoulders filled out and as the weeks passed I found I was able to work longer hours in harness. Sergeant Thunder had detailed Albert to be with me whenever I was working so that we were scarcely ever apart. But from time to time though Albert, like all the veterinary orderlies would be despatched to the front with the veterinary wagon to bring back the latest horse casualties, and then I would pine and fret, my head over the stable-door, until I heard the echoing rumble of the wheels on the cobbles and saw his cheery wave as he came in under the archway and into the yard.

In time I too went back to the war, back to the front line, back to the whine and roar of the shells that I had hoped I had left behind me for ever. Fully recovered now and the pride of Major Martin and his veterinary unit, I was often used as the lead horse in the tandem team that hauled the veterinary wagon back and forth to the front. But Albert was always with me and so I was never afraid of the guns any more. Like Topthorn before him, he seemed to sense that I needed a continual reminder that he was with me and protecting me. His soft gentle voice, his songs and his whistling tunes held me steady as the shells came down.

All the way there and back he would be talking to me to reassure me. Sometimes it would be of the war. 'David says Jerry is about finished, shot his bolt,' he said one humming summer's day as we passed line upon line of infantry and cavalry going up to the front line. We were carrying an exhausted grey mare, a water carrier that had been rescued from the mud at the front. 'Fair knocked us for six, he did, further up the line they say. But David says that that was their last gasp, that once those Yankees find their fighting legs and if we stand firm, then it could all be over by Christmas. I hope he's right, Joey. He usually is – got a lot of respect for what David says – everyone has.'

And sometimes he would talk of home and of his girl up in the village. 'Maisie Cobbledick she's called, Joey. Works in the milking parlour up Anstey's farm. And she bakes bread. Oh Joey, she bakes bread like you've never tasted before and even Mother says her pasties are the tastiest in the parish. Father says she's too good for me, but he doesn't mean it. He says it to please me. And she's got eyes, eyes as blue as cornflowers, hair as gold as ripe corn, and her skin smells like honeysuckle – 'cept when she first comes out of the dairy. I keep well away from her then. I've told her all about you, Joey. And she was the only one, the only one mind, that said I was right to come over here and find you. She didn't want me to go. Don't think that. Cried her heart out at the station when I left, so she must love me a little, mustn't she? Come on, you silly you, say something. That's the only thing I've got against you, Joey, you're the best listener I've ever known, but I never know what the divil you're thinking. You just blink your eyes and waggle those ears of yours from east to west and south to north. I wish you could talk, Joey, I really do.'

Then one evening there was terrible news from the front, news that Albert's friend, David, had been killed, along with the two horses that were hauling the veterinary wagon that day. 'A stray shell,' Albert told me as he brought in the straw for my stable. 'That's what they said it was – one stray shell out of nowhere and he's gone. I shall miss him, Joey. We shall both miss him won't we?' And he sat down in the straw in the corner of the stable. 'You know what he was, Joey, before the war? He had a fruit cart in London, outside Covent Garden. Thought the world of you, Joey. Told me so often enough. And he looked after me, Joey. Like a brother he was to me. Twenty years old. He'd his whole life ahead of him. All wasted now 'cos of one stray shell. He always told me, Joey. He'd say, "At least if I goes there'll be no one that'll miss me. Only me cart – and I can't take that with me, more's the pity." He was proud of his cart, showed me a photo of himself once stood by it. All painted it was and piled high with fruit and him standing there with a smile like a banana spread all across his face.' He looked up at me and brushed the tears from his cheeks. He spoke now through gritted teeth. 'There's just you and me left now, Joey, and I tell you we're going to get home, both of us. I'm going to ring that tenor bell again in the Church, I'm going to eat my Maisie's bread and pasties and I'm going to ride you down by the river again. David always said he was somehow sure that I'd get home, and he was right. I'm going to make him right.'

When the end of the war did come, it came swiftly, almost unexpectedly it seemed to the men around me. There was little joy, little celebration of victory, only a sense of profound relief that at last it was finished and done with. Albert left the happy cluster of men gathered together in the yard that cold November morning and strolled over to talk to me. 'Five minutes time and it'll be finished, Joey, all over. Jerry's had about enough of it, and so have we. No one really wants to go on any more. At eleven o'clock the guns will stop and then that will be that. Only wish that David could have been here to see it.'

Since David's death Albert had not been himself. I

had not once seen him smile or joke, and he often fell into prolonged brooding silences when he was with me. There was no more singing, no more whistling. I tried all that I could to comfort him, resting my head on his shoulder and nickering gently to him, but he seemed quite inconsolable. Even the news that the war was finally ending brought no light back to his eyes. The bell in the clock tower over the gateway rang out eleven times, and the men shook each other solemnly by the hand or clapped each other on the back before returning to the stables.

The fruits of victory were to prove bitter indeed for me, but to begin with the end of the war changed little. The veterinary hospital operated as it always had done, and the flow of sick and injured horses seemed rather to increase than to diminish. From the yard gate we saw the unending columns of fighting men marching jauntily back to the railway stations, and we looked on as the tanks and guns and wagons rolled by on their way home. But we were left where we were. Like the other men, Albert was becoming impatient. Like them he wanted only to get back home as quickly as possible.

Morning parade took place as usual every morning in the centre of the cobbled yard, followed by Major

Martin's inspection of the horses and stables. But one dreary, drizzling morning, with the wet cobbles shining grey in the early morning light, Major Martin did not inspect the stables as usual. Sergeant Thunder stood the men at ease and Major Martin announced the re-embarkation plans for the unit. He was finishing his short speech; 'So we shall be at Victoria station by six o'clock on Saturday evening – with any luck. Chances are you'll all be home by Christmas.'

'Permission to speak, sir?' Sergeant Thunder ventured.

'Carry on, Sergeant.'

'It's about the 'orses, sir,' Sergeant Thunder said. 'I think the men would like to know what's going to 'appen with the 'orses. Will they be with us on the same ship, sir? Or will they be coming along later?'

Major Martin shifted his feet and looked down at his boots. He spoke softly as if he did not want to be heard. 'No, Sergeant,' he said. 'I'm afraid the horses won't be coming with us at all.' There was an audible muttering of protest from the parading soldiers.

'You mean, sir,' said the Sergeant. 'You mean that they'll be coming on on a later ship?'

'No, Sergeant,' said the Major, slapping his side with his swagger stick, 'I don't mean that. I mean exactly what I said. I mean they will not be coming with us at all. The horses will be staying in France.'

''Ere, sir?' said the sergeant. 'But 'ow can they sir? Who'll be looking after them? We've got cases 'ere that need attention all day and every day.'

The major nodded, his eyes still looking at the ground. 'You'll not like what I have to tell you,' he said. 'I'm afraid a decision has been taken to sell off many of the army's horses here in France. All the horses we have here are either sick or have been sick. It's not considered worthwhile to transport them back home. My orders are to hold a horse sale here in this court-yard tomorrow morning. A notice has been posted in neighbouring towns to that effect. They are to be sold by auction.'

'Auctioned off, sir? Our 'orses to be put under the 'ammer, after all they've been through?' The sergeant spoke politely, but only just. 'But you know what that means, sir? You know what will 'appen?'

'Yes, Sergeant,' said Major Martin. 'I know what will happen to them. But there's nothing anyone can do. We're in the army, Sergeant, and I don't have to remind you that orders are orders.'

'But you know what they'll go for,' said Sergeant

Thunder, barely disguising the disgust in his voice. 'There's thousands of our 'orses out 'ere in France, sir. War veterans they are. D'you mean to say that after all they've been through, after all we've done lookin' after 'em, after all you've done, sir – that they're to end up like that? I can't believe they mean it, sir.'

'Well, I'm afraid they do,' said the major stiffly. 'Some of them may end up as you suggest – I can't deny it, Sergeant. You've every right to be indignant, every right. I'm not too happy about it myself, as you can imagine. But by tomorrow most of these horses will have been sold off, and we shall be moving out ourselves the day after. And you know, Sergeant, and I know, there's not a blind thing I can do about it.'

Albert's voice rang out across the yard. 'What, all of them, sir? Every one of them? Even Joey that we brought back from the dead? Even him?'

Major Martin said nothing, but turned on his heel and walked away.

CHAPTER 20

THERE WAS AN AIR OF DETERMINED CONSPIRACY abroad in the yard that day. Whispering groups of men in dripping greatcoats, their collars turned up to keep the rain from their necks, huddled together, their voices low and earnest. Albert seemed scarcely to notice me all day. He would neither talk to me nor even look at me but hurried through the daily routine of mucking out, haying up and grooming, in a deep and gloomy silence. I knew, as every horse in the yard knew, that we were threatened. I was torn with anxiety.

An ominous shadow had fallen on the yard that morning and not one of us could settle in our stables. When we were led out for exercise, we were jumpy and skittish and Albert, like the other soldiers, responded with impatience, jerking sharply at my halter, something I had never known him do before.

That evening the men were still talking but now Sergeant Thunder was with them and they all stood together in the darkening yard. I could just see in the last of the evening light the glint of money in their hands. Sergeant Thunder carried a small tin box which was being passed around from one to the other and I heard the clink of coins as they were dropped in. The rain had stopped now and it was a still evening so that I could just make out Sergeant Thunder's low, growling voice. 'That's the best we can do, lads,' he was saying. 'It's not a lot, but then we 'aven't got a lot, 'ave we? No one ever gets rich in this man's army. I'll do the bidding like I said – it's against orders, but I'll do it. Mind you, I'm not promising anything.' He paused and looked over his shoulder before going on. 'I'm not supposed to tell you this – the Major said not to – and make no mistake, I'm not in the 'abit of disobeying officers' orders. But we aren't at war any more, and anyway this order was more like advice, so to speak. So I'm telling you this 'cos I wouldn't like you to think badly of the major. 'E knows what's going on right enough.

Matter of fact the 'ole thing was 'is own idea. It was 'im that told me to suggest it to you in the first place. What's more, lads, 'e 's given us every penny of 'is pay that 'e 'ad saved up – every penny. It's not much but it'll 'elp. 'Course I don't 'ave to tell you that no one says a word about this, not a dicky bird. If this was to get about, then 'e goes for the 'igh jump, like all of us would. So mum's the word, clear?'

'Have you got enough, Sarge?' I could hear that it was Albert's voice speaking.

'I'm 'oping so, son,' Sergeant Thunder said, shaking the tin. 'I'm 'oping so. Now let's all of us get some shut-eye. I want you layabouts up bright and early in the morning and them 'orses looking their thundering best. It's the last thing we'll be doing for 'em, least we can do for 'em seems to me.'

And so the group dispersed, the men walking away in twos and threes, shoulders hunched against the cold, their hands deep in their greatcoat pockets. One man only was left standing by himself in the yard. He stood for a moment looking up at the sky before walking over towards my stable. I could tell it was Albert from the way he walked – it was that rolling farmer's gait with the knees never quite straightening up after each stride. He pushed back his peaked cap as he leant over the stable door. 'I've done all I can, Joey,' he said. 'We all have. I can't tell you any more 'cos I know you'd understand every word I said, and then you'd only worry yourself sick with it. This time, Joey, I can't even make you a promise like I did when Father sold you off to the army. I can't make you a promise 'cos I don't know whether I can keep it. I asked old Thunder to help and he helped. I asked the major to help and he helped. And now I've just asked God, 'cos when all's said and done, it's all up to Him. We've done all we can, that's for certain sure. I remember old Miss Wirtle telling me in Sunday School back home once: "God helps those that helps themselves". Mean old divil she was, but she knew her scriptures right enough. God bless you, Joey. Sleep tight.' And he put out his clenched fist and rubbed my muzzle, and then stroked each of my ears in turn before leaving me alone in the dark of the stables. It was the first time he had talked to me like that since the day David had been reported killed, and it warmed my heart just to listen to him.

The day dawned bright over the clock tower, throwing the long, lean shadows of the poplars beyond across the cobbles that glistened with frost. Albert was up with the others before reveille was blown, so that by the time the first buyers arrived in the yard in their carts and cars, I was fed and watered and groomed so hard that my winter coat gleamed red as I was led out into the morning sun.

The buyers were gathered in the middle of the yard, and we were led, all those that could walk, around the perimeter of the yard in a grand parade, before being brought out one by one to face the auctioneer and the buyers. I found myself waiting in my stable watching every horse in the yard being sold ahead of me. I was, it seemed, to be the last to be brought out. Distant echoes of an earlier auction sent me suddenly into a feverish sweat, but I forced myself to remember Albert's reassuring words of the night before, and in time my heart stopped racing. So when Albert led me out into the yard I was calm and easy in my stride. I had unswerving faith in him as he patted my neck gently and whispered secretly in my ear. There were audible and visible signs of approval from the buyers as he walked me round in a tight circle, bringing me at last to a standstill facing a line of red, craggy faces and grasping, greedy eyes. Then I noticed in amongst the shabby coats and hats of the buyers, the still, tall figure of Sergeant Thunder towering above them, and to one side the entire veterinary unit lined up along the wall and watching the proceedings anxiously. The bidding began.

I was clearly much in demand for the bidding was swift to start with, but as the price rose I could see more heads shaking and very soon there seemed to be only two bidders left. One was old Thunder himself, who would touch the corner of his cap with his stick, almost like a salute, to make his bid; and the other was a thin, wiry little man with weasel eyes who wore on his face a smile so full of consummate greed and evil that I could hardly bear to look at him. Still the price moved up. 'At twenty-five, twenty-six. At twenty-seven. Twenty-seven I'm bid. On my right. Twenty-seven I'm bid. Any more please? It's against the sergeant there, at twenty-seven. Any more please? He's a fine young animal, as you see. Got to be worth a lot more than this. Any more please?' But the sergeant was shaking his head now, his eyes looked down and acknowledged defeat.

'Oh God, no,' I heard Albert whisper beside me. 'Dear God, not him. He's one of them, Joey. He's been buying all morning. Old Thunder says he's the butcher from Cambrai. Please God, no.'

'Well then, if there are no more bids, I'm selling to Monsieur Cirac of Cambrai at twenty-seven English pounds. Is that all? Selling then for twenty-seven. Going, going . . .'

'Twenty-eight,' came a voice from amongst the buyers, and I saw a white haired old man leaning heavily on his stick, shuffle slowly forward through the buyers until he stood in front of them. 'I'm bidding you twenty-eight of your English pounds,' said the old man, speaking in hesitant English. 'And I'll bid for so long and so high as I need to, I advise you, sir,' he said, turning to the butcher from Cambrai. 'I advise you not to try to bid me out. For this horse I will pay one hundred English pounds if I must do. No one will have this horse except me. This is my Emilie's horse. It is hers by right.' Before he spoke her name I had not been quite sure that my eyes and ears were not deceiving me, for the old man had aged many years since I had last set eyes on him, and his voice was thinner and weaker than I remembered. But now I was sure. This was indeed Emilie's grandfather standing before me, his mouth set with grim determination, his eyes glaring around him, challenging anyone to try to outbid him. No one said a word. The butcher from Cambrai shook his head and turned away. Even the auctioneer had been stunned into silence, and there was some delay before he brought his hammer down on the table and I was sold.

CHAPTER 21

THERE WAS A LOOK OF RESIGNED DEJECTION ON Sergeant Thunder's face as he and Major Martin spoke together with Emilie's grandfather after the sale. The yard was empty now of horses and the buyers were all driving away. Albert and his friends stood around me commiserating with each other, all of them trying to comfort Albert. 'No need to worry, Albert,' one of them was saying. 'After all, could have been worse, couldn't it? I mean, a lot more'n half of our horses have gone to the butchers and that's for definite. At least we know Joey's safe enough with that old farmer man.'

'How do you know that?' Albert asked. 'How do you know he's a farmer?'

'I heard him telling old Thunder, didn't I? Heard him saying he's got a farm down in the valley. Told old Thunder that Joey would never have to work again so long as he lived. Kept rabbiting on about a girl called Emilie or something. Couldn't understand half of what he was saying.'

'Dunno what to make of him,' said Albert. 'Sounds mad as a hatter, the way he goes on. "Emilie's horse by right" – whoever she may be – isn't that what the old man said? What the divil did he mean by that? If Joey belongs to anyone by right, then he belongs to the army, and if he doesn't belong to the army, he belongs to me.'

'Better ask him yourself, Albert,' said someone else. 'Here's your chance. He's coming over this way with the major and old Thunder.'

Albert stood with his arm under my chin, his hand reaching up to scratch me behind my ear, just where he knew I liked it best. As the Major came closer though, he took his hand away, came to attention and saluted smartly. 'Begging your pardon, sir.' he said. 'I'd like to thank you for what you did, sir. I know what you did, sir, and I'm greatful. Not your fault we didn't quite make it, but thanks all the same, sir.'

'I don't know what he's talking about,' said Major Martin. 'Do you, Sergeant?'

'Can't imagine, sir,' said Sergeant Thunder. 'They get like that you know sir, these farming lads. It's 'cos they're brung up on cider instead of milk. It's true, sir, goes to their 'eads, sir. Must do, mustn't it?'

'Begging your pardon, sir,' Albert went on, puzzled by their levity. 'I'd like to ask the Frenchman, sir, since he's gone and bought my Joey. I'd like to ask him about what he said, sir, about this Emilie, or whatever she was called.'

'It's a long story,' said Major Martin, and he turned to the old man. 'Perhaps you would like to tell him yourself, Monsieur? This is the young man we were speaking of, Monsieur, the one who grew up with the horse and who came all the way to France just to look for him.'

Emilie's grandfather stood looking sternly up at my Albert from under his bushy white eyebrows, and then his face cracked suddenly and he held out his hand and smiled. Although surprised, Albert reached and shook his hand. 'So, young man. We have much in common you and I. I am French and you are Tommy. True, I am old and you are young. But we share a love for this horse, do we not? And I am told by the officer here that at home in England you are a farmer, like I am. It is the best thing to be, and I say that with the wisdom of years behind me. What do you keep on your farm?'

'Sheep, sir, mostly. A few beef cattle and some pigs,' said Albert. 'Plough a few fields of barley as well.'

'So, it was you that trained the horse to be a farm horse?' said the old man. 'You did well my son, very well. I can see the question in your eyes before you ask it, so I'll tell you how I know. You see your horse and I are old friends. He came to live with us – oh it was a long time ago now, not long after the war began. He was captured by the Germans and they used him for pulling their ambulance cart from the hospital to the front line and back again. There was with him another wonderful horse, a great shining black horse, and the two of them came to live in our farm that was near the German field hospital. My little granddaughter, Emilie, cared for them and came to love them like her own family. I was all the family she had left – the war had taken the rest. The horses lived with us for maybe a year, maybe less, maybe more – it does not matter. The Germans were kind and gave us the horses when they left, and so they became ours, Emilie's and mine. Then

178

one day they came back, different Germans, not kind like the others; they needed horses for their guns and so they took our horses away with them when they left. There was nothing I could do. After that my Emilie lost the will to live. She was a sick child anyway, but now with her family dead and her new family taken from her, she no longer had anything to live for. She just faded away and died last year. She was only fifteen years old. But before she died she made me promise her that I would find the horses somehow and look after them. I have been to many horse sales, but I have never found the other one, the black one. But now at last I have found one of them to take home and care for as I promised my Emilie.'

He leant more heavily on his stick now with both hands. He spoke slowly, choosing his words carefully. 'Tommy,' he went on. 'You are a farmer, a British farmer and you will understand that a farmer, whether he is British or French – even a Belgian farmer – never gives things away. He can never afford to. We have to live, do we not? Your Major and your Sergeant have told me how much you love this horse. They told me how every one of these men tried so hard to buy this horse. I think that is a noble thing. I think my Emilie would have liked that. I think she would understand, that she would want me to do what I will do now. I am an old man. What would I do with my Emilie's horse? He cannot grow fat in a field all his life, and soon I will be too old to look after him anyway. And if I remember him well, and I do, he loves to work, does he not? I have – how you say? – a proposition to make to you. I will sell my Emilie's horse to you.'

'Sell?' said Albert. 'But I cannot pay you enough to buy him. You must know that. We collected only twenty-six pounds between us and you paid twenty-eight pounds. How can I afford to buy him from you?'

'You do not understand, my friend,' the old man said, suppressing a chuckle. 'You do not understand at all. I will sell you this horse for one English penny, *and* for a solemn promise – that you will always love this horse as much as my Emilie did and that you will care for him until the end of his days; and more than this, I want you to tell everyone about my Emilie and about how she looked after your Joey and the great black horse when they came to live with us. You see, my friend, I want my Emilie to live on in people's hearts. I shall die soon, in a few years, no more; and then no one will remember my Emilie as she was. I have no other family left alive to remember her. She will be just a name on a gravestone that no one will read. So I want you to tell your friends at home about my Emilie. Otherwise it will be as if she had never even lived. Will you do this for me? That way she will live for ever and that is what I want. Is it a bargain between us?'

Albert said nothing for he was too moved to speak. He simply held out his hand in acceptance; but the old man ignored it, put his hands on Albert's shoulders and kissed him on both cheeks. 'Thank you,' he said. And then he turned and shook hands with every soldier in the unit and at last hobbled back and stood in front of me. 'Goodbye, my friend,' he said, and he touched me lightly on my nose with his lips. 'From Emilie,' he said, and then walked away. He had gone only a few paces before he stopped and turned around. Wagging his knobbly stick and with a mocking, accusing grin across his face, he said. 'Then it is true what we say, that there is only one thing at which the English are better than the French. They are meaner. You have not paid me my English penny, my friend.' Sergeant Thunder produced a penny from the tin and gave it to Albert, who ran over to Emilie's grandfather.

'I shall treasure it,' said the old man. 'I shall treasure it always.'

And so I came home from the war that Christmas-time with my Albert riding me up into the village, and there to greet us was the silver band from Hatherleigh and the rapturous peeling of the church bells. Both of us were received like conquering heroes, but we both knew that the real heroes had not come home, that they were lying out in France alongside Captain Nicholls, Topthorn, Friedrich, David and little Emilie.

My Albert married his Maisie Cobbledick as he said he would. But I think she never took to me, nor I to her for that matter. Perhaps it was a feeling of mutual jealousy. I went back to my work on the land with dear old Zoey who seemed ageless and tireless; and Albert took over the farm again and went back to ringing his tenor bell. He talked to me of many things after that, of his ageing father who doted on me now almost as much as on his own grandchildren, and of the vagaries of the weather and the markets, and of course about Maisie, whose crusty bread was every bit as good as he had said. But try as I might, I never got to eat any of her pasties and do you know, she never even offered me one.

After a few minutes of Q & A, segue into your sales pitch, but try not to have it perceived as such. You've got to convince the person you're meeting with that you understand his problems and his industry, that you have solutions he hasn't considered, that you can help him. At the same time, you don't want to reveal every weapon in your arsenal. So you might indicate something about the general approaches you will use, how long you think it will take to rectify the situation, what you think the benefits might be. Mention enough specifics to whet his appetite.

And don't present your ideas like a waiter reeling off the evening's specials. No one wants to hear a memorized spiel.

Act III: closing the meeting. The ideal way for the meeting to end is for the person you're meeting with to ask for your ideas in writing. This hardly ever happens. So you need to bring it up. Once you've laid out some of your ideas, you might ask, "May I follow up? Can I respond to you in writing?"

Remember: Most people want to say yes. That's why the person you're meeting with agreed to see you in the first place. By saying, I'll get this done for you, you force him either to give you the go-ahead or to say no.

Very few people are going to say no. Once they say yes, you tell them, I'll have a plan of action on your desk within a week. Can I look for a response from you shortly after that? Again, it's easier to say yes.

You have now accomplished two things. You have received the go-ahead for a plan of action. And by building in a whole train of events, you have created a feeling of confidence, a sense that things are already starting to happen.

This is the moment to bring the meeting to a close. If it goes on too long, you'll be drained of your ideas. So keep it short. Close it by saying, "Thank you, I appreciate the time you took and I'll get back to you within a week with a plan for taking this forward."

Now stand up, shake hands, and walk out.

Corporate Politics

At the first meeting, you have to convince the person you're meeting with that you can speak without the hindrance of corporate politics.

People who work inside a corporation assume that they know the corporation better than anybody, so why should they hire a consultant? The answer is easy. There are outside factors influencing the corporation that you may not understand and I can tell you how they affect you.

This approach will work on the West coast, on the East coast, and in the Middle West. It will work in Europe. It will work in Asia.

But in the South and the Southwest, people have ambivalent feelings about consultants. And once you cross into the sovereign state of Texas, you will find an attitude that's downright dismissive.

I particularly enjoy going to Texas and getting assignments for just that reason.

Show Me the Money

Note that you still haven't talked about money. Unless the client brings it up, the first meeting is probably a little early in the game, especially if the client is wavering. However, if the perspective client is desperate to hire you, discuss money now.

How much should you charge? You can charge for your time, for your analysis of a problem, or for the value you create. I prefer the last method. If I can help push a stock up several points, that's a lot of value, and I'm comfortable charging for it. If I can help an executive smooth out difficulties with a spouse—and I've been asked to do this on many occasions—that has a lot of value too. When my clients send me a check, I don't want them thinking that they're paying for my time or my thoughts: I want them to know that they're getting value.

Send a Memo

No matter how your meeting ends—with an agreement to do further business or with a series of mumbled, noncommittal comments—you need to follow up. One way to do this is to give the person something to look at. Unfortunately—as I stated before—leaving behind a brochure won't do. Sooner or later it will get thrown into the trash.

Instead, leave behind a memorandum written with this particular client in mind. It doesn't have to be exhaustive—one or two pages will do—but it has to be directed specifically to the XYZ company and it has to deal with the issues under consideration, whatever they might be.

If you have not gotten the go-ahead for writing a plan of action, sending a memo gives you another chance to hook your potential client.

If you have gotten the go-ahead, you might still want to write the memo. Use the words "Strictly confidential" on the envelope, and send it to the person you met. You can be sure that person will look at it: Everybody wants to see something that's confidential.

At the top of the paper state that this memo is intended to take company XYZ to a level that it doesn't currently enjoy. Then summarize your ideas. Remember: Keep it short. And make certain that every aspect of the memo relates to the company.

This memo will solidify your position.

The Power Behind the Phone

The memo needs to arrive at the office within two or three days of your meeting. If you are also planning to submit a plan of action, the memo needs to arrive a few days prior to that. The whole process shouldn't take more than a week.

During that crucial time, call the secretary regularly to let her know the progress that you're making. Tell her, you'll have something for her boss in short order. You want her to be your ally. Enlist her assistance now.

Don't Write a Proposal

Let me be blunt: Hardly anybody writes proposals and succeeds. Maybe that's because the word proposal sounds tentative. The person reading it is going to think, I suppose I should make a decision. But perhaps I ought to look at other proposals first.

Instead, write a plan of action. It sounds more direct, more effective. If you're presenting someone with a plan of action, you're saying, this is something you can do right now and I can work with you on it.

That semantic shift may sound minor but it produces a more positive, action-oriented mind set.

Writing a Plan of Action

When writing a plan of action, put in defined goals that will benefit the person receiving your plan. You want that person to think, I can look good if this consultant does this for me.

It's best to emphasize actions that will produce immediate results, especially for the person you're working with.

You also want to include the following:

- one or more specific objectives
- an analysis of the company's current situation
- a series of actions that will help the company reach your stated goal by a certain date
- an estimate of how long each action should take
- a discussion of the likely results of each action
- an acknowledgment of possible problems that could arise
- and a clear explanation of your fee and how you expect to receive it

The Art of Making Presentations

When you present the plan of action, try not to send it through the mail. You're better off presenting it in an ordinary meeting.

When you sit down for the first part of the meeting, wait for the other person to speak. If that doesn't happen right away, fine. Let the silence fill the room.

They have invited you in to make your presentation. Since you're not saying anything, they have to do it. The chances are they're going to say something that's positive for you. That's what you want.

That positive statement sets the tone and enables you to start on the best possible note. In my experience, that means jumping to the finish line by stating the ultimate result that you hope to achieve. Try saying something like this:

- I want to put points on the board for XYZ Company
- I can help raise the productivity of XYZ Company
- I can help you navigate through a transition
- I can help you create a product turnaround

You want that headline to be in everyone's mind throughout your presentation. That way, as you discuss your various ideas, everyone knows where you're heading.

As you go through your plan of action, be sure to ask questions. You want to say, Does that work for you? How does that sound to you? Can I have some feedback on that? By asking those questions, you engage the other people in the discussion.

The worst thing to do is to sit down and read through your plan of action while they sit there in judgment. At the end they will say thank you, good-bye, we'll think about it. And you know what that means.

You have to engage them in the process.

Contracts with Clients

A lot of people are reluctant to ask for contracts. I'm not sure why, but I think they're afraid that if they ask for one, the client might back out.

I think they're foolish. A contract is your protection. But I realize that asking for one can be intimidating. This is what I recommend: Instead of whipping out a twenty-page legal document written in six-point type, tell your client that you'd like to formalize your agreement. You can say, I'm going to send you a note and I'd appreciate your acknowldgement of it. That's all you have to do.

The note, which will lay out the terms you have discussed, can be your contract. It should list what you are going to do, how long it will take, how much you expect to be paid, and so on. Be sure that the contract has an exit clause.

You might also include a clause that says this contract will continue for thirty days past the completion date unless canceled by either party in writing. That gives you thirty days to generate more business.

Solving Problems

Once you've written your plan of action and signed the contract, you have to prove yourself by actually solving your client's problem. Doing that requires a mixture of skills. To wit:

- It takes the ability to understand what the problem actually is. That means objectively analyzing the situation by stepping outside your client's range of understanding and being able to offer a new perspective on the situation.
- It takes the courage to be candid about the problems facing the company.
- It takes the creativity to develop a series of possible solutions.
- It takes intelligence and compassion to guide the client through the process. That's not so hard while things are going well. But when you're delivering bad news, it's another story.

Bring in the Hessians

Consultants are like mercenary soldiers: They are hired to perform tasks that no one else wants to touch. They speak the truth, even when it's ugly. That's probably the least enjoyable part of a consultant's job—and the most important. To do it effectively, you have to be soft with the client. When you tell them they have to fire half the people on their payroll, or declare bankruptcy, or do anything else that's unpleasant, it helps to relate a funny story to lighten the burden. You have to convince them, even when things are unimaginably bad, that things are not as bad as they could be. There's a real art to it.

You may be tempted at those moments to emphasize the optimistic view and underplay the negative. Don't do it. The ideal consultant has the courage of his or her convictions and tells the client what the client ought to know.

Keeping the Ball in the Air

One advantage of being a consultant is that each situation is unique, so you're always doing something new. The boredom quotient is low.

One disadvantage is that every time you complete the task for which you were hired, you're out of work.

To keep from being constantly on the job market, you need to turn one-time clients into on-going clients. That process begins with the successful completion of your first assignment. Once you've done that, you've established a platform. You can say to your client, we've got a toehold. Now how do we go to the next level?

In other words, you enter into a process with the client. A process is never completed. If it was, we'd all be in Nirvana, smoking cigars and drinking cognac. In this world, there's always something you can do better. That's the way business is—and it doesn't matter if you're running a mom-and-pop bodega or General Electric.

That's why, with every client I have, I try to meet with them regularly to evaluate what has happened and to look to the future. There's constant reassessment: Here's what worked, here's what didn't work, here are the lessons we learned from it, and here's the plan for the next month or two.

You should always have a clear view of where this client should be in two or three years. In every meeting you should be saying, here's how I can take you forward over the next few weeks toward that vision.

To do that effectively, you need to build upon your successes and accept failure when it comes (because ideas that sound great in the office don't necessarily hold up in the marketplace). You need to think purposefully and creatively. Most of all, you need to make sure that the ball is always in the air.

Back to Emerson

There comes a time in the life of every successful consultant when everything begins to fall into place.

By then you will have learned how to generate work. You will no longer be surprised when new assignments arrive at unexpected times and from unlikely sources. You will know immediately which clients you are going to enjoy working with and which ones are going to cause you trouble. And once you accept a project, you will understand intuitively what the next step ought to be and you will know how to make it happen.

Until then, remember the words of Ralph Waldo Emerson, who pointed out (in an essay entitled "Wealth") that "good luck is another word for tenacity of purpose."

8

A PR Primer

A young writer recently got into trouble for being ungracious. Oprah Winfrey had chosen his novel for her book club. Although every single book so designated has become a best seller and made its creator rich, the young author was not happy about it. He felt uncomfortable and ambivalent—would he be taken seriously in the literary world?—and he expressed those feelings to a reporter.

Not surprisingly, his uneasiness soon became public knowledge and he was roundly criticized. Ms. Winfrey withdrew her invitation to appear on the show. Other writers derided him as offensively elitist. An op-ed piece in the *New York Times* heralded him as the "Not-Yet-Ready-for-Prime-Time Novelist" and described the whole brouhaha as one in which the novelist "puts foot in mouth, chews hard, then swallows."

Did sales suffer? Frankly, I don't think they did. But the author's personal reputation certainly did. And although he tried to apologize, apologies—as any PR person could tell you—are always too little, too late.

That's why it's so important to present yourself to the public in the right way, right from the start. You don't need to hire a PR agent to do that. Just use your common sense—and read this chapter.

What Is PR?

Many people think of public relations as a sort of synonym for media exposure. Without a doubt, media exposure is a major concern for people in my field. But PR can also be described more generally as the way the public perceives you, whether you're talking to Oprah or to the person sitting next to you on the train. If you interact with the public on any level, public relations affects you. That's why you need to pay attention to it—even if you've also hired a guy like me to help you out.

How to Develop Your Message

Part of doing your own PR is simply knowing what to say about yourself when the occasion arises. Some people evidently think that the occasion arises whenever another person is in the room. Not so. One of the worst PR mistakes you can make is to talk about yourself all the time. But there are times when you should talk about yourself, and when these situations arise, you need to be prepared. You can do that by writing out three separate spiels about yourself:

The twenty-second elevator speech. Imagine the circumstances. There you are, heading to the twenty-sixth floor, when who should enter the elevator but the very person you have been trying desperately to meet. What should you say?

At that tense moment, you don't have time to compose a speech in your head. It should be there, ready to go: your Twenty-Second Elevator Speech, a nutshell description of your most important qualities and experiences.

The one-minute presentation. Or maybe you're at a convention or a cocktail party, and you figure you can talk about yourself for about a minute. What would you say during those critical sixty seconds? Don't trust yourself to speak extemporaneously: You run the risk of talking for too long or of getting sidetracked. You want to have your one-minute statement permanently filed in your brain, ready to go.

The written essay. Finally, there's the 1,500 word essay, an in-depth story about yourself. I would begin it with eight to ten topic

sentences. Think of the topic sentences as headlines, and keep them short and punchy.

Then apply the old-fashioned principles of composition, the ones you learned in school: supply two or three examples to illustrate each topic sentence.

This exercise will organize your thoughts and enable you to talk about yourself at length when the situation calls for it. It also provides a sort of backstory for briefer presentations. Thus, if you need to limit your message to three or four items, you can pick and choose from among the points in your essay.

Recently, for example, a woman came to me to prepare for a television interview. She's a powerful woman, but she was nervous. She asked me, what should I say?

I said, write down three major points you want to make. Then let's put together two examples for each one of those points. That's what you should say about yourself. It's that simple.

She took my suggestion, and her television appearance was a smashing success.

Have ever wondered what kind of advice you might get if you hired a public relations person? Now you know.

Why You Should Do Your Own PR

I once had a highly accomplished client who did remarkable work but was so hesitant to do any form of PR, for reasons that are still a mystery to me, that I don't even feel free to tell you what field he was in. Suffice it to say that had he wanted to be known, he would be famous. And admired.

He came to me because he was involved in a project that ran into difficulties and he wanted the problem to go away. He said, it's your job to keep this out of the press.

I said, okay, we can minimize the damage. But what we really should do is to draw attention to the many successful projects you've worked on that have nothing to do with this catastrophe.

He never accepted that part of the equation. He believed that his work spoke for itself. I said, yes, but if you don't point it out to people, they won't notice it. He said, they will. I said, they won't. We argued back and forth.

Ultimately, it was his call. Which is why you've never heard of this guy.

Even if you feel sympathetic to his approach, you can't afford to emulate him, because PR concerns your reputation, which is constantly in flux, constantly being recreated, whether you do anything about it or not. If you refuse to participate in the process, you risk finding out, too late, that your image has changed and your glorious accomplishments have faded into memory.

You don't want to become someone about whom it might be said, "She used to be quite capable. I don't know what she's doing these days."

Not after fifty, you don't.

If you still have a hankering for recognition, if success in the world still means something to you, then refusing to do your own PR is a huge mistake.

The Ten Commandments of Public Relations

I don't compare myself to Moses, but I do know something about PR. These are the basic rules:

Commandment Number 1: Have a Clear Message

What do you want to impart to people about yourself or your business? It can't be ten different things. A message that complicated distorts the process and is too much for people to absorb. To do effective PR, for yourself or for anybody else, you have to limit yourself to three or four messages, tops.

You might, for instance, want people to think of you as industrious, honest, and an expert in your field. You might want to be viewed as someone who can motivate others. You might want to be seen as an original thinker or a compelling leader or someone with an uncanny grasp of the economy. These are important messages and they can be very effective, assuming you obey the next two commandments.

Commandment Number 2: Support Your Message With Examples

If you pride yourself on being able to get the job done on time,

even under intense pressure, you better have several examples of how you did just that.

If you want to be known as someone who can motivate people, you have to have examples of how you've increased productivity where you've worked in the past.

In short, you had better be able to prove your case.

Commandment Number 3: Remember Your Audience

To craft an effective message, make sure the messages you choose resonate with your audience. Observe them carefully and consider the qualities that matter to them—not just to you.

I know a widely-published professor who had a year-long appointment at an ivy league university, at the end of which he was to be granted tenure. During the year, he spoke at international conferences. He wrote for a prestigious journal. His students gave him a standing ovation at the end of the term, and he dazzled the faculty with his artistic, linguistic, and culinary talents, none of which had anything to do with his major field of expertise. Yet despite his efforts, he didn't get tenure.

Why? Because what people say they want is not necessarily what they really want. Sure, if you had asked the faculty, they would probably have said they were looking for someone who was a brilliant scholar and a charismatic teacher. The professor was trying to give exactly them that. His message was clear: I am a star.

Unfortunately, that message did not resonate with his audience. They didn't want a star. They didn't want to feel upstaged. They wanted a colleague, a committee member, someone who would fit seamlessly into their community. A better message would have been "I am a team player."

Commandment Number 4: Repeat Your Message Again and Again

Take it from me, the PR you do on Tuesday is forgotten on Wednesday. To drive your message home, your campaign has to last over an extended period of time. Otherwise your message won't sink in. Unless you can provide people with repeated examples of what you're doing, you will fail to make an impression. People forget.

If you have any question about that, conduct a little test right now. Ask yourself, What was on the front page of the newspaper one week ago? Or how about this: What was on the television news two nights ago? Very few people can answer either question.

Plus, you've got to remember that you're dealing with the passing parade. The group you're communicating with today will have an entirely different composition two years from now.

So you've got to repeat your message over and over, in different ways. One iteration is never enough.

Commandment Number 5: Establish Yourself as an Expert

Are you an expert on crisis management, on maritime law, on antiquarian books, or, for that matter, on anything at all? If so, you're in an ideal position to do your own PR.

Just the other day, a fellow called us. He said that in this current economy, there are going to be more bankruptcies than ever and I know how to help companies who are facing that problem.

None of my clients is close to bankruptcy, but he put the idea in my head, and I made an appointment to talk with him. I may never need to recommend his services. But if I do, I'll call him. Because even though I know plenty of lawyers and accountants who are knowledgeable about the intricacies of bankruptcy proceedings, this guy has established himself as an expert in my mind. I'd call him first.

The trouble with being a generalist is that it means you're almost never the perfect person for the job. By becoming an expert at something, you become the perfect person.

Many people resist this idea because they are afraid of getting pigeon-holed. They think that if they become an expert on, say, growing organic lettuce, they'll never be allowed to talk about the rest of the vegetable kingdom. Actually, it's the other way around: By concentrating your expertise, you give your professional life a focus.

In my profession, for instance, I concentrate on the public relations needs of CEOs around the world. Sure, I have clients who don't fit that category. But the bulk of my work comes to me because I have established my expertise in a certain area.

To establish yourself as an expert, you need to give your work a focus. You need to have the courage to proclaim yourself an expert. And you need to be able to back up your claim.

One way to do that is to act upon the corollary to this commandment.

Corollary to Commandment Number 5: Create a Newsletter

There is no easier, faster way to establish your credentials as an expert than producing a newsletter that puts out information other people can use. And it doesn't matter what your field is.

If I ran a janitorial service, for instance, I would send out a regular newsletter about trends in cleaning. If I owned a shoe store, I'd develop a newsletter about shoes. If I was a waiter, I'd create a newsletter about trends in eating out.

Do I follow my own advice? In this case, yes. Since my work focuses on the business community, I've developed a newsletter about the issues that are of concern to them: Mainly social, economic, and political trends. It's called the *Dilenschneider Trend Forecasting Report*. It comes out in January and September, enabling me to keep in contact with about 2,000 people.

That may not sound like a lot. But people regularly quote from the *Dilenschneider Trend Letter,* often verbatim. Just the other day, I talked to a man who said he'd like 500 copies of the *Trend Letter* to send to his clients. And last year, Paine Webber used several parts of the *Trend Letter* in presentations all over the world. I couldn't have hoped for a better third-party endorsement.

Another benefit of writing the *Trend Letter* is that it creates a dialogue with my clients. I've found that the real indication of whether or not people read it is whether they contact me to argue about it.

For instance, take global warming. I think it's a problem. That hole in the ozone layer worries me. But many people think those concerns are misguided. Every year, I get letters from representatives of big oil companies arguing with me.

Same thing happens with the Japanese business community. Every year, evidently, I get something wrong. Every year, they send people to see me so we can discuss it.

Does this please me? You bet. I'm always willing to consider the evidence and I'm happy to engage in a debate. It involves everyone in a constructive exchange.

Besides, it's great PR.

Commandment Number 6: Control Your Output

As many a beleaguered celebrity and public official can attest, it's easy to lose control over your message, and once that has happened, it's hard to get it back. That's why it's important to try to do whatever you do in as controlled a way as possible, especially when you're dealing with media or the public.

For instance, maybe you're going to give a speech. You need to make certain that every aspect of your presentation, from the way you dress to the way you answer questions at the end, supports your overall message.

Maybe you need to clear up a misunderstanding. You could leave a message over the phone, but we all know how dangerous that is. Or you could write a letter. That way, you take control of your own communication.

When you give a speech, write an article, or send someone a letter, you take control of your own message. That's a good thing.

Commandment Number 7: Have Someone Else Do It for You

I don't mean hire someone. I mean that the most desirable PR always comes from someone else's mouth. You need a third party to sing your praises.

Of course, we all know people who are only too happy to do it themselves. They do it incessantly—in conversation, in writing, and even in interior decoration. My favorite expression of the how-great-I-am syndrome is the love-me room, which is invariably decorated with degrees and awards and trophies and framed book jackets and photographs of the Great One hobnobbing with celebrities or bowing to the Queen, all vivid ways of showing how important they are. I guess this is their way of reinforcing themselves.

I have to say, some people evidently succeed by doing this. You've probably spent as many miserable hours in their company as I have. But I persist in believing that the same folks would be more successful—not to mention more popular—if they could only quiet down. Bragging is not good PR.

Having other people talk about you in a positive way is good PR. The third party is extremely important.

That's why artists, actors, and writers have agents. That's why the best way to meet someone is to get somebody else to introduce you and the best way to get a job is to be recommended.

And that's why there is ultimately nothing more important in terms of PR than your network.

Commandment Number 8: Expand Your Network

New York's Shea Stadium is named after a great man named Bill Shea, who ran a law firm called Shea and Gould. He was the king of the networkers. On his desk he kept seven or eight huge Rolodexes filled with names and addresses from all over the country. His assistant kept the information up to date so that Bill could keep in constant contact with these people. His networking skills enabled him to become a very powerful person.

It's never too late to expand your own network. After all, this is not something to do once in a while. You need to do it all the time. The number one way is by going to events. Go to trade associations, professional events, conferences. Attend university events, charity functions, and community meetings. Be visible.

And talk to everyone. When you meet people, think about how they fit into your design for going forward—and think about what you can do to help them. (For suggestions on how to start a conversation, see Chapter 10.)

After you meet someone, you can write a letter that says I met you at the church festival last week. I found our conversation about such-and-such quite fascinating and I'd like to continue it. May I call you? Most people are flattered.

Don't be heavy-handed about expanding your network, though. I've seen people do that firsthand. My wife and I like to throw big parties. More than once, I've had people call me afterwards to ask for a list of every person who attended. I always demur. It's an embarrassing moment.

On the other hand, people come to parties at my house and meet other guests and get together afterwards, and I think that's fine. That's the way it should be.

Another way to network is to get the people you already know to introduce you to the people you want to know. To do this, you have to ask, and that's not easy. But you have to do it.

For instance, let's say you're looking for a job. And let's say you've done some volunteer work for the Cancer Society. I guarantee you, someone you've worked with there can introduce you to the members of the board of the Cancer Society, who undoubtedly include some influential people. It's hard to make such a request. But it's an easy way to expand your network and get some great advice.

Finally, there's one other way to expand your network, and it's the easiest of all. Be nice. To everyone. From the moment you get up to the moment you go to bed, you probably have dozens of interactions that you don't normally record: with people over the phone, people who come to the door, people on the street, people at lunch. If you're decent to these people and you keep an eye out for how you can help them, your network will expand.

The word "networking" has come to have a negative tinge because it has been associated with ambitious, status-conscious careerists who only care what you can do for them. People who go about networking in that way ultimately make very few solid connections.

Building a network in the right way means being willing to go beyond yourself.

Commandment Number 9: Follow Up

Return your phone calls. Write thank you notes. Reciprocate. And do it with dispatch.

Obvious advice? Obviously. But too many people don't do it.

For instance, I met an interior decorator at a dinner party about a year ago It was fascinating sitting next to her and I told her how much I enjoyed it. I also told her that I knew a couple who had just purchased an enormous house. I said, I know they would benefit from working with someone of your abilities. Please call me and I'll put you in touch with them.

Four or five months later, she called. By then it was too late. The moral is clear: Follow up—and do it quickly.

Commandment Number 10: Use the Media to Your Advantage

There's a maxim that as long as they spell my name correctly, any PR is good PR. I don't agree. If the press writes a negative story about you, that's not good. You have to be careful about how you expose yourself to the press and what you say in the presence of a reporter, something the young novelist I discussed at the top of this chapter seemed to forget.

Many people have the notion that it would be great to get a story into the press about themselves. In my view, you never want to get a story into the press about yourself. That's because good reporters strive for balance and objectivity. So if a reporter writes a story about you, it will mention your failings as well as your accomplishments, quote your detractors, and remind everyone of that long-ago scandal. That kind of coverage—the only kind you're going to get in a halfway respectable publication—is not going to help you, because people tend to remember the negatives more than the positives.

The best way to appear in the press is to comment about a topic, never about yourself. That way, even if people disagree with you, you're engaged in a legitimate argument over a point of view. You are not the center of attention. And yet attention naturally flows to you. It's a PR coup.

Using the Media

You don't need to be well-known to use the media. You just have to be savvy.

Let's say, for instance, that you're an expert in library science or bilingual education or the housing needs of the elderly. (That is, you're a librarian, a teacher, or a real estate broker.) You can go on the internet, do a search, and get the names of scores—make that hundreds—of writers who have addressed that topic in the last year.

You'll know where they are, how to spell their names, what they wrote about. Then you can write them a letter. I'd say, I admired your recent piece in the *Arizona Republic*. Your analysis impressed me and I wonder if you've considered such-and-such. You might offer them a relevant anecdote from your experience or a piece of information they didn't know.

They may not answer your letter. Don't let that bother you. Next time they run a related story, send another letter. Your aim is to establish yourself as an expert, a source of information. If your letters are thoughtful, sooner or later the reporter is likely to contact you.

Or consider writing letters to the editor. Every time there's a newspaper story about your topic, write a letter to the editor. There are basic rules for writing letters to the editor. We all know them:

- A letter to the editor has to be short and to the point
- It has to be timely
- And it has to present a point of view that is different from the opinion expressed in the original article

Admittedly, it is difficult—though not impossible—to get letters to the editor published in prestigious papers like the *New York Times* or the *Washington Post*. It can be easier to break into smaller papers. Fortunately, it doesn't matter where your letter is published. Because afterwards, you can Xerox it and send it to your network with a brief note. The *Citizen Register* took the time to publish this letter, you can say. I think this topic is extremely important, and I thought you'd be interested too. Any comments? You'll get comments back and that creates a dialogue.

Anybody can do this.

Appearing on talk radio is something else almost anybody can do. You can certainly call call-in shows, although I don't necessarily recommend that. Or you can find out who the producer of the show is and contact that person. If you present yourself as someone with expertise and a point of view, the producer may be interested.

One of the easiest ways to get on the air is to write a book. Send it to radio and TV stations along with a set of questions you can answer.

You can also appear on television shows. But don't do it if you don't look good. I don't mean you have to look like a movie star. But you have to look okay.

If you do end up on television, please dress appropriately. Men look better in a jacket and tie. Women look better in a suit or a dress. Avoid complicated prints. Avoid casual clothes. Don't look like you're dressed for the *Jerry Springer Show*, even if you are.

One of the great things about radio and television is that their needs are inexhaustible. They have to put guests on the air all the time. If you're inventive enough, you ought to be able to figure out a way to take advantage of that.

If you find yourself going on TV, the most important person to talk to is not the host. It's the camera man. Get there early so you can talk to him about getting the most flattering camera angle. If you've got a weight problem—and remember, TV will exacerbate that—try to get a head-and-shoulders shot.

Finally, if you're anxious, contact a media coach. Some of them are pretty good. But many are hacks who will try to change you. Don't let them do it. You are who you are and you want to express your point of view.

PR Don'ts

There are certain dangers inherent in doing your own PR. Most of them can be avoided. Here are PR's dirty dozen for the over-fifty crowd:

Bad taste. I think that speaks for itself.

Trying too hard. Calling someone repeatedly or communicating without a valid reason is a mistake. If people don't respond after two or three well-spaced attempts, back off.

Insulting people. Insulting somebody, even subtly, is a mistake, and sometimes it can be a worse one than you realize. The person you insult, however inadvertently, may say nothing to you. But they could denigrate you to everyone they know. They could even repeat your remark, allowing an insult to one person to ripple out and insult an entire network. That's not a good thing.

Lying. The problem with lying is that when people find out about it—and they do—no one will ever trust you again.

A friend of mine encouraged a mutual acquaintance to see a film called *Run, Lola, Run.* Our acquaintance rented the film from Blockbuster but never got around to watching it. Nonetheless, he wrote my friend a letter in which he said that *Run, Lola, Run* was a great film. Thrilled, my friend immediately called to discuss the film in detail. "Did you like that scene halfway through?" he asked. But our acquaintance couldn't relate to it. He was caught in a lie.

That was a bad mistake. It had repercussions. Yet it was entirely avoidable.

Opportunism. Being opportunistic at the wrong time can turn a viable business prospect into a PR catastrophe. The appearance of benefiting from someone else's misfortune makes people queasy and can besmirch your reputation. Don't do it.

Presenting yourself poorly. If you come across as a slob, people will think of you that way. If you *seem* disorganized, people will assume that you *are* disorganized. As you should know by now, everyone judges a book by its cover. Present yourself according.

Writing badly. Be judicious in your writing. Use the spell check. And proofread everything you intend to send, preferably by printing it out and reading a hard copy. It's amazing how easy it is to miss the most blatant errors when you're reading them on a computer screen.

If you're unsure of writing fundamentals, show your résumé and any important letters to someone whose editing skills you trust.

Finally, read *The Elements of Style* by William Strunk Jr. and E. B. White or, for a more contemporary take, *Woe is I: The Grammarphobe's Guide to Better English in Plain English* by Patricia T. O'Conner.

Being bigoted. Making ethnic jokes, racial slurs, or sexist comments is never okay, even when you think it is. Not only is it the wrong thing to do, but from the PR standpoint, it's a disaster. I'll never forget eating dinner with a group of high-ranking military officers in San Antonio. As we walked out of the restaurant, a United States Army colonel made a joke about the African American waiters. It was greeted with dead silence. A few minutes later, the general said, I've had a lot of black soldiers under my command and some of them died for their country.

He never said, that was the wrong thing to say. But he left that point on the table. Making bigoted remarks is not only immoral—it's just plain dumb.

Associating with negative symbols. Many people drink, but associating yourself with alcohol is not smart. You don't want people to be reminded of you every time they see a vodka ad.

The same is true with tobacco. Many people smoke, but you don't want people thinking of you every time they see a pack of Marlboro Lights.

I'm not saying you can't indulge in those activities. But I think it's smart to wait for someone else to recommend them first, particularly when you're looking for a job or otherwise trying to impress.

People judge you by what you do, where you do it, and whom you do it with. So be aware.

Being out of date. A lot of older people don't understand new trends and are not interested in them, especially when they involve music and television. For example, *The Simpsons* has been a top-rated show since 1989. Just now, I asked a fifty-seven-year-old friend of mine if he'd ever seen it. The answer? No.

That's a mistake.

Different generations have different concerns. You can start a conversation with anyone in my generation by asking, where were you when John F. Kennedy was shot? But the business world is filled with heavy-hitters who weren't even born in 1963. No point in asking the question.

If you're going to talk about events from your youth—I would avoid it if possible—you've got to relate them to the present. Otherwise, it's just an exercise in nostalgia, which is never interesting to anyone who wasn't there.

I take as my model an Englishman named Alan Campbell Johnson who'd been with Mountbatten in India. After World War Two, he handled the transfer of power from the British to the Indians. When he discussed that period of time, he never spoke about how great he was, although he was. He talked about what we had learned and how it could be applied to international situations today. He wasn't reliving the past; he was applying the lessons of the past to the present. That's a very different thing.

Being bitter. It's understandable that people over fifty sometimes feel bitter. Letting it show, however, is a mistake. I remember counseling a man who came in wanting a job. His first comment was that he figured he was too old and didn't have much of a chance but he was going to try anyway.

That was a strike against him. Making a comment like that is, at best, pointless. At worst, it introduces the thought that maybe you *are* too old. My advice: Keep those thoughts to yourself.

Trying to hide your age. Trying to look good for your age is a worthy goal; being coy about your age or pretending to be significantly younger than you actually are is a mistake.

Sooner or later, you'll slip up and your true age will be revealed—whereupon it will become a topic of conversation. Avoid that embarrassment entirely by being, if not forthcoming, then at least not dishonest about your age.

Spin vs. Substance

In the last decade or so, public relations has come under criticism, thanks to the notorious concept of spin. But spin, no matter how expertly done, eventually comes to a sputtering halt.

What matters is substance. You have to have something to say. You have to develop expertise. You have to be associated with something that matters.

That's the key to doing your own PR.

9

Bridging the Generation Gap

"Old Age and Youth cannot live together," wrote Shakespeare, who lived at a time when fifty was considered old.

Sometimes, it seems to me, they can't *work* together either. The assumptions and experiences of the Baby Boomers, now in their forties and fifties, and the so-called Silent Generation, which preceded the Boom, differ dramatically from those of Generation-X and the yet-to-be-named generations snapping at their heels. Those differences create tension.

In the past, all this had relatively little impact in the workplace because each generation was locked into its own organizational stratum. Top management slots were filled by the most experienced people, who were invariably the oldest; middle management positions were filled by the next generation; entry-level jobs went to the youngest generation. You started on the bottom when you were young and spent the rest of your career "climbing the corporate ladder." It was that simple.

In many companies today, that ladder has been kicked aside and the rigid hierarchies of the past have been overturned. In addition, young entrepreneurs in their thirties and even in their twenties have altered the business landscape by building companies that are immune to the old rules. So things are different. Older people may have more experience and a greater sense of loyalty, but younger people have an edge they didn't have in the past. Not only are they more flexible and energetic, the eternal attributes of youth, they are vastly more knowledgeable in one essential area—technology. That gives them a serious advantage.

Young people today are not afraid to ask for what they want, and they have high expectations. In fact, according to a survey of college seniors taken by KPMG International, 74 percent of them believe that they will become millionaires.

Plus, they expect to get there in record time. I wouldn't be surprised if a sizeable number of them expect to reach that goal by age thirty.

Neither my generation nor the Baby Boomers entertained expectations like that. Those of us who aspired to become part of the establishment—far from a universal goal in the 1960s and 1970s—thought it would take a while. We figured that we'd follow the rules and if we were up to snuff, the rewards would come in due time.

Generation-Xers don't want to wait. And who can blame them?

Generational Stereotypes

Ever since Tom Brokaw wrote a book about the men and women who fought in World War II and titled it *The Greatest Generation* (a term immediately embraced by all to whom it applied), subsequent generations have taken a beating. Unless you happen to be a member of that exalted generation, don't expect to hear anything good about yourself.

Thus people my age, born just before the Baby Boomers, are generally characterized as dull conformists (unless they qualify as members of the Beat Generation, in which case they are considered conformists of another sort). Baby Boomers are viewed as self-satisfied egotists. Generation-Xers are seen as apolitical slackers who mistake irony for intelligence. One way or another, everybody gets slammed.

In the real world, that kind of stereotyping—like any other kind—won't wash. No single individual embodies all the clichés of a generation. Still, there are generational differences. So let me begin with the harshest of them: The younger generation thinks you're old. And they're right. They think you look tired, out of shape, and pathetically out of style. They're dismissive of your musical tastes and contemptuous of your computer skills. If you come from the generation before the Baby Boom, they think you're authoritarian, conservative, and way too enamored of World War Two and the heroes of the past. They don't want to hear another word about Winston Churchill or the Brooklyn Dodgers.

If you're a Baby Boomer, you get a flogging that's more severe. Ever wonder why younger people are so pessimistic and cynical? It's because of you! Young people think that you're self-aggrandizing, self-righteous, self-indulgent, and probably to blame for every major problem facing us today. You could have become enlightened. You could have cleaned up the environment and changed the world. But you didn't. Instead, according to a thirty-year-old newspaperman of my acquaintance, you became just another boring businessperson obsessed with PowerPoint displays and contemporary business clichés. (In contrast, he noted, members of the Greatest Generation make statements that mean something.)

And by the way, members of Generation-X do not want to hear another word about the 1960s, much as they envy you for having lived through that tumultuous era. Anything you might say about those fraught, unforgettable times only hurts you because it reminds them that you're a sell-out. After all, once upon a time you had ideals. But Baby, look at you now.

There is not a lot you can do to change these views. Even responding to such criticisms plays against you, as I realized the other night when I watched several beleaguered Baby Boomers valiantly trying to stand up for themselves. The thirty-year-old at the table looked at me wryly. "Note the defensiveness of the Baby Boom Generation," he said.

Yet the younger generation wants everything that you want, including love, money, personal fulfillment, and success in their chosen fields. They just don't want to wait for it the way you did.

Your job, if you want to get along with them, is to help them get what they want—not to prove how misguided they are. The first step in the process is to understand something about them.

Mission impossible? Not at all.

How to Get Along With Younger Generations

Sooner or later, you will find yourself having a professional discussion with someone who is twenty-five or thirty years younger than you, young enough to be your child. And yet you will be talking to that person as an equal.

That person could be your customer, your client, even your supervisor. That person could be someone you're interviewing or someone who's interviewing you. Here's how to hit it off:

Don't patronize. Don't pander. They can see through that kind of condescension, and they don't like it.

At the same time, recognize that young people need encouragement, sometimes in ways that will strike you as distressingly childish. A museum official put it this way:

Muhammad Ali once described someone by saying, "He has some maturities on him." I think of that often because I've noticed that young people, especially the men, need more attention than older people and are more demanding. Right now, I'm working with two people who are installing a new exhibit. The younger one, who's in his mid-twenties, has a strong need for personal attention and constant interaction. Last week, he literally asked me to watch him do something and then take his picture while he was doing it. The other one, who's about ten years older, only consults me when he needs direction. He respects the fact that I'm going to make the final decision, the considered judgment. He doesn't waste my time. He's got some maturities on him.

Nonetheless, she gives the younger employee a good deal of attention. She figures—and I think she's right—that it'll pay off in the long run. When dealing with young people, it's important to withhold judgment and make that investment.

Understand that by virtue of living over half a century, you have gained a historical viewpoint. Within your field, for instance, you have some idea of what has worked and what hasn't. You know that some efforts sound good but fail miserably while others are hugely effective but take time. You know that traumatic events can throw everything into chaos. And you know that, as a rule, chaos subsides and order returns. Young people don't—can't—know that.

The movements of history are also unknown to many young people. Even those who have studied history—a distressingly small number, as far as I can see—lack a visceral understanding of its rhythms.

In the weeks following the events of September 11, young people were profoundly shaken. In an article in the *New York Times*, reporter Jane Gross addressed this phenomenon. She pointed out that the Greatest Generation remembers Hitler. Baby Boomers remember air-raid drills and the Cuban Missile Crisis. But Generation-X experienced none of those calamitous public traumas, and as a result, many were unprepared to deal with our latest one.

If you're in touch with young people, part of your role is helping them understand the forces of history and come to grips with the realities of our time.

Don't try to fit into their milieu. I don't mean you should avoid their milieu. On the contrary: I recommend seeking out their milieu. But pretending that you belong there, hoping that they'll see you as one of them, will only earn their contempt. Better to think of yourself as a tourist in the country of the young.

Once in a while, when I'm in the city late after a television appearance, I'll stop in at a club on the way home. I'll sit at the bar and have a cup of coffee and chat with the young people milling around. I don't know whether it's the music or the conversation, but I am always stunned to realize how different their perspective is from mine. Being with them, in however casual a way, helps me feel more in touch. I know many uptight business executives, dark blue suit types, who would never do that, and I think it stultifies their lives and their careers.

Build their confidence. To do that, you need to understand that no matter how confident young people pretend to be, they are riddled with insecurities, even when they are hugely successful. You have to be able to deal with those doubts.

One way to help them feel more confident is to share your knowledge. Many times, younger people are put into supervisory positions by top managers and urged to fly on their own.

Unfortunately, they don't have the depth of experience to do that. When you see a young person in that position, you have an opportunity to help. First, understand that you're not in the running for that job, whether you want it or not. So you're not a threat. Second, recognize that you have an opportunity to transfer your experience to the younger person in a way that may ultimately help you. I've seen it happen.

I knew a wonderful older man at an insurance company who had a supervisor almost thirty years younger than himself. Some older people in that situation might feel bitter. This man took the opposite approach. He assisted the younger man every step of the way, never seeking praise for himself, always seeking to advance the other fellow. Over the years, these two men forged a bond, with the older man imparting to the younger man everything he knew about business. In time the younger man became the company CEO. When that happened, he took excellent care of the older man.

That's not a reason the reason to extend yourself. You should do it because it's the right thing to do. Still, it's nice to know that doing the right thing sometimes pays off.

Understand that what motivates young people is not what motivates you. For instance, you may be motivated by working with a team. Younger people may find it more exciting to work independently. Your goals, interests, and turn-offs are not theirs. And it's a sad fact that the stories it has taken you a lifetime to accumulate are of little interest to the younger generation.

I know a man in his seventies who still has not figured this out, even though he has ten children in their teens and twenties. He's a wonderful story teller, a real raconteur. I sit in rapt attention when he talks. His children listen politely—that's the way they were raised—and leave the room at the first possible moment. They resent his need to be the center of attention, and they don't relate to the stories he tells.

That doesn't have to happen. Stories told in a vacuum drive young people crazy. They don't want to hear about it. On the other hand, they're hungry for ways to think about their own lives and challenges. That's why stories you tell young people should always relate to the present. If there's something in it for them, they'll listen.

Recognize that younger people want to do things fast. They seek instant gratification. You've learned the importance of patience and deliberation. They have not. If you insist upon doing things your way, you'll be happy, but they'll be hopping up and down with frustration. Neither of you will benefit.

I'm sympathetic to the young in this regard, because I remember when I was a young man in a hurry. I wanted to open new offices and hire people and offer new services, and I drove my boss crazy. He repeatedly told me not to push him. I felt that my ideas were good ones, and it frustrated me to be dismissed so cavalierly—so I kept trying. In response, he would occasionally tell me to do a quality assurance study, or to get a second or third opinion, or even to write a paper on one of my ideas. This truly frustrated me. I didn't want to write a paper. I wanted to see my idea bear fruit in the real world. There was a serious standoff between the two of us.

In retrospect, I can see what a pain in the neck I probably was. I can also see how he could have dealt with me more effectively. All he had to do was to sit down and talk with me about my ideas and their consequences. Had he done that, I believe I would have understood that the implications of these ideas were more multidimensional that I realized. We never had those discussions, and so I became resentful and it was a problem.

Today, I meet plenty of young people who are eager to leap into the fire, and I'm the one who has to slow them down. The way to do that, I have learned, is to respond immediately. So I generally suggest that we go downstairs, have a cup of coffee, and discuss the idea. I say, you've got the kernel of something important here, let's see if we can make it work. In the process of having that discussion, we both generally learn whether there is something there. And frequently they come to the conclusion that there's nothing there. Which is fine. But if you don't discuss it with them, you don't get to that point of resolution.

Listen. Consider the possibility that, despite their inexperience, young people might actually have something to say. My sixteen-year-old son, Geoffrey, has complained that older people seldom recognize that fact. "They believe that kids don't have opinions," he told me. "It's really aggravating. They think I'm not old enough to think. Excuse me? I'm thinking! Hello!"

Unfortunately, listening has become a lost art. Most people don't understand that there's strategy and skill in simply listening to what people say. They want to do all the talking.

To get along with younger people, you have to stifle that urge. I believe that it's important for me to sit with my two sons and their friends and listen to what's on their minds. Sounds easy. It's not, because when Froot Loops are getting scattered across the table, you automatically want to pick them up. The minute you do so, the conversation ends.

In the workplace, where your younger colleagues are in their twenties and thirties, Froot Loops are presumably not an issue. But the same rules apply. You need to listen with an open mind. You need to postpone your urge to make momentous pronounce-ments or to lob small criticisms their way—and that includes criti-cisms couched as suggestions. You need to listen without judgment.

Ask questions. Deep in their hearts young people recognize that they don't know it all. The best way to help them is to ask a series of constructive questions about who they are and what they want to do. Then let them reach their own conclusions.

Young people will benefit from this because, if you ask ques-tions in the right way, they will be encouraged to consider various courses of action. You will benefit too because talking to young people about their lives (and the lives of their friends) can be un-believably illuminating.

I remember talking with a wealthy, successful, thoroughly con-fused twenty-something. Her father had arranged the meeting in hopes that I could help her figure out what lay ahead for her.

She and I met for breakfast at a restaurant on the ground floor of the building where I work. I told her that every New Year's Eve I sit down and make a list of my goals and priorities. I asked, what would you write down if you were going to make such a list?

She couldn't answer that question but it led us into a discus-sion that helped her focus. I know she left that meeting feeling good about it because between the time when I left the restaurant and the time when I arrived at my office, which is on the twenty-sixth floor, she had called her father on her cell phone and he had called me to say what a terrific meeting it was. I was happy and relieved.

However, I will admit that during the meeting itself, I was careful to order a cappuccino rather than my usual glass of juice. I didn't want her to think I was too, too uncool.

Never betray their confidences. I work with a lot of young people, some of whom are quite prominent. I always begin by telling them that I will never betray their confidences. You and I can discuss any issue under the sun, I say. If you need to talk in the middle of the night, if some terrible problem is weighing you down, I'm here to help. I will work through the matter with you and it will never become public knowledge. I maintain strict confidentiality.

That declaration helps to build a bond of trust.

Keep up. This is an essential part of getting along with the young. You have to be tuned in to the present. In my mind, that's a 24/7 process.

One aspect of keeping up is media awareness, beginning with newspapers and magazines. I try to read a wide variety of periodicals. They include, among others, the *New York Times,* the *Wall Street Journal, Barron's, USA Today,* the *Village Voice, Foreign Affairs, Sports Illustrated, Fortune, Business Week, Fast Company,* and the *Utne Reader,* which offers a collection of articles from the alternative press.

I try to flip through *U.S. News and World Report, Time,* and *Newsweek* every week. I start from the back. I read the daily papers closely, so I skip the news summaries in the front. But the back of the book often contains deeper, more thoughtful stuff and I think that's one way to keep up.

I also try to be aware of what's on the best seller lists, what's hot on Broadway, what the significant art shows in town are. I make an effort to catch the majority of the movies that receive Oscar nominations. I try to watch major television shows, at least once. I even keep up with popular music. Not that it's difficult: My twelve-year-old son, Peter, has definite opinions on the subject and he keeps me up to date.

Another important way of keeping up has to do with talking to people—lots and lots of people.

I talk to strangers all the time. For example, when I go to the Yankee game, I make a point of visiting with the security guard and of having a beer in the Yankee Club with a bunch of fans who are probably truck drivers. I will ask what's going on in their lives. That may sound like an intrusive question, but I assure you, most people seem happy to answer it. I ask questions all the time of people who are outside of my usual sphere. I talk to people in planes, trains, and automobiles, not to mention elevators. Yesterday, for instance, I talked to a messenger in the elevator. I asked him what it was like going between tall buildings in a time of heightened security and he gave me his point of view, which was interesting—and not what I would have expected. I also asked him what he was listening to on his headphones, and he answered that too.

Tap the power of biography. Young people want role models, though they seldom admit to it. That role model might be you—but unless you are one impressive human being, it might not be. A better bet for them is to find a public figure, someone they can read about and emulate, if only in a limited fashion.

Recently I spoke to a young woman about the late Katherine Graham, publisher of the *Washington Post*. Kay Graham arrived at a place in life that was extraordinary for her generation and she did it with style and conviction. The young woman wasn't convinced. She said, "I'm not Katherine Graham."

I said, "That's right. But you can learn some lessons from Katherine Graham." Reluctantly, the young woman agreed to read *Personal History*, Graham's Pulitzer Prize-winning autobiography. We went through the whole book and literally picked out a dozen lessons that were helpful for this individual.

I also know a young man who wanted to be a heavy hitter in the area of venture capital technology. I said, let's dissect the life of Warren Buffett. Oh, no, he said. He didn't want to be like Buffett.

I said, I know that. But Buffett conducted himself in ways that are important for you to understand. For example, Buffett chose to invest in staples, items everyone wanted to have like Coca-Cola or razor blades. In his business life, he made it a point to give responsibility to others. He kept checks on them, but he also empowered them. Those are two lessons you can apply in your own life.

I guess I convinced him, because this guy literally went out and bought all the books about Warren Buffett he could find. He didn't try to develop himself as Warren Buffett—that wasn't his goal—but I'd say he was influenced by seven or eight ideas that Buffett used to guide his life and his business. Reading the book was a thought-provoking experience.

Accept the changing of the guard. That means being willing to help younger people succeed, even when they're placed in positions above you—a situation that's as awkward for them as it is for you. I know of a company that recently went through a period of upheaval. In the midst of it, a group of older people walked into the younger supervisor's office and, to his astonishment, announced that they were there to help. We have some ideas to offer, they said, but we want you to know that, whether you accept them or not, we're behind you. The younger person was knocked off his chair. He accepted their help; they accepted his authority; the company flourished.

Mentoring

One of the best ways to connect with the younger generation is to become a mentor to a younger person. Another way to do it is to allow a younger person to become a mentor to you. Either way, mentoring is a time-honored way to impart information and to connect one generation with the next.

When I graduated from Notre Dame with my Bachelor of Arts degree, I didn't know what to do. So I asked my father. We sat in my bedroom late one night and he said to me, you have three choices. You can join the army. I can help get you a job in a local department store selling shoes. Or you can go to graduate school.

That made it easy. I said, I want to go to graduate school. My father then suggested I talk to a journalism professor named Walter Seifert. So one day I showed up at his house. My timing wasn't good: Seifert's daughter was preparing for her wedding, and everyone was involved in a rehearsal. He didn't even invite me in.

He just met me in the driveway, handed me a stack of papers he had written, and said, I don't have a lot of time to spend with you, but take these and read them.

Spurred on by the less-than-thrilling options my dad had laid out, I read everything Seifert gave me. When I went back to see him, we developed a relationship that lasted until his death. (In fact, I gave the eulogy at his funeral.) As my first mentor, he propelled me into my career. Even as I became more seasoned in my business, I continued to ask him for advice. He made a huge impact on my life, and I'll never forget him.

After I started working, other people also became mentors to me. One of them was a colleague in his late sixties. He dropped by my apartment every morning and we walked to work together. On the way, he would discuss sports and politics and, most of all, business. What he was really doing was teaching me lessons that he thought were important. He was smart enough to know that he had to tell me these things in a low-key, off-hand way that would be easy for me to accept. He figured out exactly how to do it. He was extraordinary.

Another man who was tremendously helpful to me was my supervisor, who was twenty-four years my senior. After work, we'd walk uptown together. For four years, we walked about fifty blocks in good weather and in bad. Occasionally we'd stop for a cup of coffee or a drink, and every step of the way he was talking to me about leadership, about literature, about all kinds things he thought I should know. Not everything filtered through. But a lot did, and I owe him for that. He understood precisely what he was trying to do, and he was very helpful to me. I've never forgotten his generosity.

Thanks to those experiences, I know how important it can be for a young person to have an older mentor. When a young person comes to me, either formally or informally, for guidance, I remember what I learned from the people who were my mentors, and I try to pass it on.

At the same time, my days of being mentored are not over. I think it's important to be mentored by people who are older, younger, and in entirely different fields. If you're entering a new business or beginning a new job, an older mentor—or in any case, a more experienced one—can show you the ropes.

But an older mentor is unlikely to have a handle on the younger generation. That's why I recommend having a younger mentor— and the older you are, the younger your mentor should be. A younger mentor can give you insight into what's hot, what's happening, how business operates today, how young people think.

Fortunately, it's not difficult to find a younger mentor. Here are a few ways to do it:

Look for someone at work. Keep in mind that you don't have to announce that you want that person to be a mentor. In fact, it's best not to, especially if the person is significantly younger than you: It sounds too intimidating. But you can certainly find someone to ask for advice or opinions, and I think that's a smart thing to do.

From time to time I eat lunch with a younger man who works in my building. We'll pick up a couple of hotdogs from a vendor and sit together on a bench. I don't ask him how to run my business. But over the years, he's given me a lot of insight into how younger people think, and that has been very helpful.

Take a night class at a college or university, and look for a young professor—or another adult student—with whom you might be able to connect.

Work with a trainer. That might mean a career coach. But it could also mean a physical trainer, someone who can talk to you in an out-of-the-box way while you're on the treadmill. It's a given that not all of those well-muscled young people are up to the job of advising, in which case you shouldn't bother. But quite a few of them are. I've been surprised recently by the number of people who have quoted their trainers to me. It made me think about the nature of being a mentor. What does it require, really? Sometimes all a mentor needs to be is a sounding board with a sensible mind and the ability to motivate, which is precisely what trainers do for a living.

Join a group that includes younger people, and seek them out. I have made it a habit to extend myself to the Public Relations Society of America and the International Association of Business Communicators as a speaker or program participant, partly because it's an easy way to meet the younger people in my profession. I don't want to become a dinosaur in my own field. Hearing their ideas, watching their responses, and talking with them helps keep me current.

And I may be wrong, but I think they enjoy sharing their thoughts with someone as obviously senior as myself.

Being a Mentor

Finding someone to mentor is easy. Anyone who seeks your advice is an automatic candidate. But you have to approach the relationship carefully.

Ever try to cram information down someone's throat? Ever try to convince a young person who is inexperienced in precisely the area of your greatest expertise that his or her goals are unreachable? Then you know how difficult mentoring can be.

To be an effective mentor, it helps to follow these principles:

- Don't be authoritarian. Rule number one.
- Have something to say, and keep it short. It's best to think in terms of headlines when you're mentoring somebody. Let them come to you for the details.
- Be informal. My mentors walked me up the street and down the street. We talked over coffee. Our encounters were never a big deal. By making them formal or uptight, by delivering facts and lessons, you risk turning a mentoring session into an uncomfortable tutorial. And no one wants that.
- Do not give orders. Do not say, this is the way it's done. No one likes to be told what to do, but young people are especially adverse to it.
- Don't take slights personally. When an uncomfortable topic comes up, young people are likely to push back or close down the discussion, sometimes in ways that hurt your feelings. Don't let it.
- Tell stories. You've got to jolly people along when you're mentoring. One way to do that is through telling stories. That way you can make your point, even about the most difficult

personal issues, without being confrontational. Sometimes it helps to be oblique.

- Always use humor.
- Be lavish with praise. Give people full credit for every contribution they make, however minor. It's the best way to keep the discussion alive.
- Despite repeated opportunities, never say, *I told you so.*
- Remember that younger people don't share your attitudes, even about mentoring. In *Generations at Work,* authors Ron Zemke, Claire Raines, and Bob Filipczak explore those differences. "Boomers," they write, "like mentors because they think it will them put on the promotional fast track. Xers like mentors because they are a kind of surrogate parent, someone who cares about them and will support them." It might be wise to keep those differences in mind, and act accordingly.
- Set boundaries. No matter how generous your intentions or how great the need, there's only so much you can do.

A Last Word

When I was young, I was sure of one thing: I did not want to lead a narrow, constricted life. Like every English major who has ever lived, I was affected by T. S. Eliot's great poem, "The Love Song of J. Alfred Prufrock." You remember him: he's the guy who measured out his life with coffee spoons and wondered, "Do I dare?"

I was determined not to turn into him. I wanted to have adventures, to take risks, to mingle with stimulating people, to see the world. And I have.

But I have become aware in the last few years that it's easy, as we get older, to pull back, to stop reaching out to new people or visiting new places or contemplating new ideas. I don't want that to happen to me.

I want my world to continue to expand. One way to make sure that happens is to maintain an open dialogue with the young.

10

Getting Back in the Game

Maybe you love your career but you've suffered a few setbacks. Maybe you decided, in one of those bleak moments that descend upon everyone once in a while, that your entire career has been a mistake and you should start all over again. Or maybe, after years of waiting for the proper moment, you've decided to dismiss your doubts and pursue your dream. Whatever your situation may be, it's not too late—it's never too late—to begin anew.

Yet these are troubled times. Millions of people in the United States are out of work and unemployment is approaching levels that we haven't experienced in generations. I've seen direct evidence of it. The Manhattan office of The Dilenschneider Group is on the same floor as Lee Hecht Harrison, an important outplacement firm. More than once in the months since September 11, I have gone to the washroom that we share and seen grown men literally bent over the sink crying because they have lost their jobs. It's a tragic situation.

Nor are we the only ones with economic troubles. With France and Germany facing similar problems, it doesn't look as if we'll climb out of this for a while. You would be foolish to consider a career change without acknowledging this reality.

Nonetheless, despite everything, I don't believe we're entering a dark age. I believe we're standing on the brink of the unknown, and we'll meet the challenge. As a people, we are inventive, alert, capable of finding opportunities even in the worst of times. I'm certain that in the years ahead, men and women around the world will come up with creative ideas and innovative products that will make life safer, easier, more fun. It's inevitable. The human spirit cannot resist the lure of invention.

Which is why, if I were contemplating a career move, I would draw up my plans in as careful a way as possible and launch my ship.

Here are the eight basic rules for starting—or restarting—a career, no matter what your age is and no matter what's going on in the world.

Rule Number 1. Find a Focus . . . or Fake It

Wanting to create change is not enough. You need to know what you want to do, and you have to be able to articulate it with some degree of specificity. For many people, this is not a problem. They know exactly what they want to do and they're passionate about it.

But a surprising number of people, for one reason or another, don't have a clue. They would love to commit themselves to a career, if only they could figure out what it should be. But every profession they can imagine has a downside, and so they feel paralyzed.

If this dilemma is affecting your life, you might consider talking to a career counselor or reading one of the many books that address this issue. (The classic in this genre is probably Marsha Sinetar's *Do What You Love, The Money Will Follow: Discovering Your Right Livelihood.*)

Books can be enormously helpful. But ultimately, only you can make a decision. When in doubt, trust your intuition. Most of the time, it will tell you which path to choose.

But if you can't seem to access that inner knowing, if you're lost in a fog of confusion, and simply can't make up your mind, I have one simple piece of advice: Jump in. Choose. Flip a coin if you must. And then give your all to whatever your choice may be.

True, every new venture has its drawbacks, and you will undoubtedly suffer from them. But you're already suffering. Better to take action and see what happens than to sit around waiting for inspiration to strike. Besides, allowing yourself to wallow in uncertainty seldom leads to clarity. It is just another form of procrastination.

As former Beatle George Harrison sang (in a song I hadn't heard until after his death), "If you don't know where you're going, any road will get you there."

Rule Number 2. Be Resolved

Without absolute resolve, you're unlikely to get anywhere. Getting back into the game is a lot of work, and you're sure to take a few knocks along the way. If you're not committed, don't waste your time. You'll only disappoint yourself.

For instance, I know a talented woman in her fifties who has had half a dozen careers since she passed the half-century mark. She's been a caterer, a party planner, a realtor, and several other occupations. But because she lacks resolve, she's flitted from one area to another and her success has been limited. Her frustration and bitterness leak out into her social contacts. As a result, people don't particularly enjoy her company, and she feels—correctly— that she hasn't gotten back into the game.

I've met a lot of people like that. They throw themselves into their new careers with enthusiasm. They rent fabulous offices, send out announcements, and distribute their new business cards, with the snappy logos and memorable e-mail addresses, to everyone. But the first time they hit a glitch or a slow period, they lose their determination and give up. My advice: Don't do that. Find something to focus on and, having done that, be resolved.

Rule Number 3. Set a Goal

Perhaps the most important step is setting a goal. Not a vague, feel-good goal; not an unrealistically ambitious goal; but a doable, reachable, specific goal.

This process is not the same for a person over fifty as it is for a younger person. A thirty-year-old person who's floundering may feel like time is passing him by. In reality (as we now see), time's on his side.

Time's on your side too, but in a different way. Because you don't have a lot of it to waste, you're ready to use your time effectively. You know how pointless and counterproductive it would be to set goals that will take twenty years to achieve.

That's why I recommend fine-tuning your goal into something that you can reasonably expect to achieve in two or three years.

To do so, you may want to quantify your goal, as many experts recommend. How much money can you realistically expect to earn in any given period of time? How many articles can you hope to publish? How many new clients can you attract? Writing down the numbers will help you know where you're heading and when you can expect to get there.

Rule Number 4. Make a Plan

Once you have a focus and a goal, the next step is to develop a step-by-step plan of action. This plan, especially if it involves a foray into new territory, will not work out in the way you're imagining. Over time, it will mutate in unpredictable ways. Even so, you have to map it out and act on it.

Begin by generating a list of everything you will need to do to make your goal a reality. Once you've listed a couple of dozen actions, prioritize them. Estimate how long each one should take and set up a schedule, complete with dates. You may want to write up a formal business plan, if only because the discipline that requires will encourage you to think things through as realistically as possible.

Your plan tells you where you should be now, three months from now, and a year from now. It provides an overview. Once you have that, you're ready to begin the work-a-day efforts that can carry you from here to there.

Rule Number 5. Use To-Do Lists

Is there a successful person on the face of the earth who doesn't make lists? I've never met one. In addition to your plan of action, which takes the long view, I recommend two kinds of To-Do lists:

- A weekly list, with a maximum of three or four goals. The purpose of this list is to keep you focused. It should concentrate on the main activities that will get you closer to your goal. So keep it short. A list of 117 items cannot possibly keep you on track.
- A daily list. Want to get mired in minutiae? This is the place. But don't forget to look at your weekly list first and to prioritize.

Rule Number 6. Take Action

Writing something on a list, as everyone knows, is a far cry from actually doing it. At some point, you have to act. But what if you don't know where to begin?

I discussed this with Carol Kinsey Goman, Ph.D. She has been successful as a nightclub performer, a therapist, a writer, and a communications consultant. In that last capacity, she has addressed groups in nineteen different countries and worked with virtually every industry on the planet. She has a deep understanding of the issues involved in career change, and her comments were on the money:

You know, people get paralyzed. They wonder, what if this isn't what I should be doing? But it doesn't matter if it's the wrong thing. It doesn't matter. Get out there and take a step. Go in some direction. I've always been a fan of energy, and I think that if you get into action, the energy will snowball. Just do something.

Rule Number 7. Let People Know You're Starting

No matter how remarkable your product or service may be, you'll never get a seat at the cabaret if people don't know what you're doing. To launch your business successfully, you need to inform people in as many ways as possible. Have you compiled a mailing list of prospects and people who will recommend prospects? Have you sent out an announcement? Have you put out a press release in the local paper? Have you given a talk at your local service club?

Maybe that sounds like a waste of effort. Yet that's how Carol Kinsey Goman kick-started her career as a therapist:

> When I opened my business, I was divorced and broke, and I thought, no one will know I'm here. I don't have any money to advertise, the Yellow Pages have already been printed, and there is no way on earth that people are going to know that this office is open. So I thought, I'll speak to the Kiwanis and the Rotary Club and the Lions Club and any other luncheon group that brings in free speakers, just to let them know I'm here.
>
> I was working with hypnosis and doing a lot of work with athletes, and I thought that might interest men because I could talk about golf. I was also doing non-smoking and weight control, and I decided that would make a good luncheon speech. So I began to attract clients. One thing led to another, and my therapy practice took off.

Rule Number 8. Celebrate

You'll know you're making progress when you start passing milestones. Those milestones might be: developing a business plan, having a productive conversation with an influential person, getting a new client, signing a lease, publishing an article, giving a speech . . . you name it. Only you can decide which events qualify as milestones.

And only you can decide how best to celebrate them. I cannot emphasize enough how essential this part of the plan is. When you pass a milestone, seize the moment! You should say to yourself, I've done something important, I've fulfilled a goal, and it's time to celebrate.

Do something that makes you feel good. Go to dinner. Get together with a friend. Treat yourself to a book you've been wanting to read. If the milestone is relatively insignificant, acknowledge it in an appropriately small way. (I know a consultant who celebrates minor triumphs by sitting down at the piano and playing a Strauss waltz.) If the milestone is a major one, pull out the stops.

I know a fellow in South Florida who rewards himself when he reaches a goal by taking a dozen of his friends to a Chinese restaurant. At the start of the meal, he stands up and announces that he has succeeded against all odds and has called his friends together to celebrate with him. He has fun at these dinners but more important, they reinforce the accomplishment, which is the purpose of the celebration.

Asking for Help: The Don'ts

Most people are afraid of feeling foolish, afraid of being rejected, and too insecure to admit their weaknesses and ask for assistance. So they don't get the help they need.

But almost everybody is willing to assist if they're asked in the right way and at the right time. As someone who gives advice for a living and thoroughly enjoys the process, I can tell you that being asked in a sincere way feels good. I'm thrilled when I can make a positive difference in someone's life. When that happens, I feel validated as a human being—and I believe that most people feel the same way. If you understand that, you can tap into the experience of accomplished people and find precisely the help you need.

Unfortunately, many people don't know how to ask for help effectively, as I've had ample opportunity to learn. Here's how to avoid the most common mistakes:

Don't ask for something the other person cannot—or does not want—to give. In my case, I know a lot of powerful people. Many of them are my clients—my private clients. So you can imagine how uncomfortable I feel when folks I barely know ask if I can introduce them to those accomplished, busy people. Believe me, requests like that don't make me want to help. They make me want to sneak out of the room.

Don't ask for too much. Keep your requests reasonable. I'm thinking of one man who has asked me for help—on more than one occasion, I might add—by saying that he'd like me to give him advice, to give him business leads, to introduce him to people and, worst of all, to critique his work. To be blunt, that's baloney! It's a lot of work for me with no payoff in sight. That's not the kind of help I want to deliver, and I don't think I'm unique that way. When you ask for help, you want to make sure the person doesn't feel you're going to be a burden.

Don't ask for an overview of the field. Like many people, I'm not a fan of informational interviews. Aside from the fact that they are time-consuming, there is something disingenuous about them. I always suspect that, really, the people who request these interviews are hoping to be offered jobs. Since I know I'm bound to disappoint them, I'd just as soon avoid these interviews entirely. When I do agree to see someone as a courtesy, I give a pat presentation which surveys the field of public relations and public affairs in about seven or eight minutes. After that, there's nothing more to say.

Twenty or thirty years ago, these interviews may have served a purpose. Thanks to the internet, they no longer do. Don't ask someone else to do your homework. It's a turn-off. Plus, you don't want to waste a valuable contact by asking for something you can get easily on your own.

Don't ask in an arrogant way. This infuriates people. The underlying feeling is one of entitlement: "I deserve to have this information (or this money or this job). I shouldn't even have to ask." This is not a winning approach.

Don't beg. Presenting yourself in a pitiful way does not engender sympathy. It makes people cringe.

Don't ask for money. That's what banks (and parents) are for.

Don't ask for something that will require a huge investment of time.

Don't abuse someone else's personal time by asking for help at night, on the weekend, or on a holiday. Don't be an intrusion. Call at a time when it's convenient for them.

Don't push too hard. You need to apply some pressure, but tread lightly. You don't want the other person to dread the sound of your voice.

Asking for Help: The Social Contract

The key to asking for helping is giving the people you're asking the sense that helping you will benefit them. That can occur in many ways. They can benefit psychologically by feeling that they're doing a good deed. They can benefit because they're enlarging their network through you. They can even benefit monetarily.

A total stranger, someone who found my name through a professional association, once asked for my help, and I agreed to give it, gratis. He updated me daily on his job search, and I responded with tips, advice, analysis. Little did I know, though, that our dialogue would continue for about two years. Many times, I was sorry I'd signed on to this. But to my surprise, it ultimately paid off—for both of us. He got a great job and hired me as a consultant to his new employer. That was a tremendous reward.

Recently, a young man who had been referred by a top executive at *Reader's Digest* came to me for help. He impressed me because, unlike so many other people, he didn't just sit there, pleading. Instead, he had all kinds of ideas about how he could help me if I helped him. That made me want to help him more.

When you need help, think in terms of how you can benefit the people you ask. Otherwise, why should they bother?

How to Ask for Help

Here's how you can maximize your chances of getting the help you need:

Keep your request short, your approach business-like, and your demeanor upbeat.

Make the person you ask feel important. You don't want to be insincere or devious or sycophantic. But let's face it: Flattery works. If nothing else, you can say you're a person who is known for helping others. I appreciate that. I know that you've extended yourself to others many times, and people admire you for that. I need your help now.

Ask for something that's actionable—not just some data that you're going to write down in your palm pilot and stash away for all eternity. You want the other person to do something for you that will generate movement and lead to something else. You want to create linkage.

Ask for a contact or referral. You can say, Who can I talk to? If the person draws a blank (which rarely happens), rephrase the question. Ask, Is there anybody in this field who could help me take the next step? Is there someone who is knowledgeable about such-and-such? Sooner or later, if the person you're talking to is in the loop, he or she will pony up. Then you ask, What's the best way to contact that person? Can I use your name? Questions like that—specific and easy-to-answer—will produce results.

Let the person know that you intend to reciprocate. Even if it's the first time you've met, you can say, I've heard a lot about you. I hope that this is a relationship that goes on for many years, and I can tell you, I remember the people who have helped me and I intend to reciprocate.

It's possible that the people you say that to won't believe you. They may dismiss your words as a bravura performance. More likely, they'll admire your attitude (assuming you are sincere) and decide to help.

Let the person know that you need the help within a certain time frame. Say that you need the help in one week or two weeks or a month, and ask if you can check back in. If there's a specific opportunity in front of you, you might say that you need to act on it quickly. People are more likely to help you out when they have a sense of immediacy.

Offer assistance, especially if your request is a complicated one. Offer to draft the letter, to address the envelopes, to coordinate with the secretary, to make phone calls, to do whatever research is necessary, and so forth. Make it easy on the other person.

Say that you're missing only one more piece of the puzzle. It's discouraging to be asked to help when you know that dozens of things will have to happen before the goal is in sight. But it's hard to say no if the person asking is already most of the way there. People feel guilty saying no in an instance like that—a fact that you can use to your advantage.

Let the people you're asking know that you will spread the news. This is especially effective if you have friends in common. Everybody wants to have a positive image. Let them know that helping you will generate good publicity.

Nail the sale. Before you leave, say something like, What's the next step? Or, How do we begin? You should never leave the room without asking for the order. If you ask, the person has a hard time saying no.

What should you do if the person says, can we put this on hold? Sure, you say, We can. But there is a compelling reason why we should take action now. Without in any way projecting an image of desperation, be prepared with a convincing reason for making a move immediately. Never let a person off the hook too easily. After all, you're probably not going to have a second chance. You've got to succeed the first time you go to the plate.

Send thank you notes immediately. And as soon as you can, return the favor.

Who You Know

You've heard the old adage, it's not what you know, it's who you know. I'd like to dispute it. In all honesty, I cannot. I've seen too many examples of people who skim by on a modicum of talent shored up by a Rolodex of gargantuan proportions and a busy social schedule. The truth is that knowing the right people is enormously helpful. That's why, if you're hoping to change your life, you need to expand your circle. It isn't easy, though—especially if, like 50 percent of the population, you consider yourself shy.

By the time most people hit their fifties, they have conquered the worst aspects of their shyness. But high-stress events can bring those excruciating feelings back. That's what happened to a client of mine. She is a highly accomplished businesswoman who even gets invited to the White House from time to time. But it wasn't doing her much good, because whenever she got invited to an important event, she lost all her confidence and would find an excuse to back out.

For several month after I started working with her, I didn't understand why she behaved in such a self-destructive way. I wondered whether her inability to enjoy and take advantage of social occasions indicated a serious psychological weakness. Eventually I realized that it did not. The problem was simply insecurity.

I noticed that, like most people, she did fine once a conversation got going. The difficulty came when she had to initiate a conversation, particularly in a situation where she felt ill at ease—like the White House.

Fortunately, she was able to get a handle on her anxiety once she knew how to present herself (see Chapter 3) and how to start a conversation.

How to Start a Conversation

Large gatherings, whether they are professional conferences, charity balls, or PTA meetings, are an excellent way to meet people—in theory. In reality, breaking into established groups can be incredibly difficult.

I speak from experience. I'm not generally a shy person (you can't be in the business I'm in if you're shy), but I've had my moments nonetheless.

For instance, when I was in my thirties, I was invited to the Chicago Club for their "Renewal," an annual event, held the first Saturday in January, during which members gather around a groaning board laden with wild boar and roast turkey, to welcome the New Year. The members were influential people who were important to me in my business, and I was thrilled to be invited. Yet I felt overcome by a wave of awkwardness and discomfort. I dealt with it in the traditional way: I spent a lot of time hanging up my coat, a lot of time making sure that I looked okay, a lot of time chatting with the doorman. I didn't want to mix, and when I finally tried to conquer my unexpected shyness, the club members were standing in tight circles and I couldn't break in.

I was wasting an opportunity. So I developed a bunch of questions and forced myself to approach a few club members. Soon I found myself in the midst of conversations.

How can you start a conversation with a stranger? Eschew hardball questions. Avoid negative remarks. Keep your political opinions to yourself, at least for the moment. Above all, make it easy. Here's how:

- Look around. Get oriented. Get something to drink, alcoholic or otherwise. If you don't know anyone, approach someone who's alone and introduce yourself. Or join a group that has gathered into a loose, casual circle. (Avoid groups standing in physically tight circles because it will be hard to break into them.) After a few minutes, enter the conversation by responding to a comment made by one of the other people in the group.
- Comment on the immediate environment. Better yet, ask a question about it. Doesn't the doorman Felix do a terrific job? And did you know that he's been here for twenty-five years? Isn't the food terrific? Isn't it wonderful to hear those Christmas carols? Phrase your question in a way that is likely to elicit a positive response.
- Ask about a local phenomenon such as the traffic, the weather, or—best of all—a local sports team. Are the Bears going to do the job this Sunday? How do you think the coach is doing? This technique generally fires up a conversation in about three seconds. If it does not, be prepared with a backup question. Worse comes to worst, you can revert to the perennial question: How do you know our hostess? Or . . .
- Comment on the news—but not on the front page. When you read the paper in the morning, find an obscure but intriguing article, something on page sixteen that the other person is unlikely to have seen. If it relates to an interest you share (such as a professional or civic association to which you both

belong), so much the better. Again, keep the tone of the conversation upbeat.

What if, despite all your efforts, you can't get a conversation off the ground? Or what if your fellow party-goer responds negatively to everything? What if he says that Felix is a moron, the food is inedible, Christmas is nothing but an exercise in excess, and the coach should be fired?

My first suggestion is to move on, because connecting with this person isn't going to be fun. Or you could stand your ground by saying that Felix is a nice guy; that the shrimp dumplings are delicious; and that yes, Christmas is often too commercialized, but this year it's different because . . .

Exchanges like these may sound dumb, but they work. They worked for me that long-ago day in the Chicago club. I fell into conversation with a much older man, who finally said, you're new here, let me introduce you around. My confidence zoomed. Later he proposed that I sit next to him at lunch. From that day on, my life in Chicago opened up, and I came to feel truly at home in the Windy City.

Hot Tip

The suggestions given above are easy ways to break the ice. But clearly there's more to be said on the subject. One expert who says it well is Susan RoAne. Her best-selling book *How to Work a Room: The Ultimate Guide to Savvy Socializing in Person and Online* tells you how to get into a conversation, how to get out of one, and more. I recommend it.

Looking Ahead

I have been accused of being a pessimist. I reject that view. I think I'm a realist. But be prepared: You may not like what I'm about to say.

Here it is: One of these days, you're going to look in the mirror and be appalled. Your health is going to falter. Terrible losses could afflict your personal life. Unexpected competition could kill your business. At some point, like it or not, you may even have to retire—and that, in my opinion, is never a good thing.

And then there's terrorism, global warming, and the state of the economy. In times like these, there is reason to worry.

Yet that's where people in their fifties and sixties (and beyond in many cases) have the edge. We're old enough to have developed perspective and coping skills. We long ago came to a recognition, however rueful, of both our abilities and our shortcomings. We are experienced enough to define our goals realistically, energetic enough to pursue them, and wise enough—or battered enough— to recognize the necessity of finding balance.

I think that's a privileged position to be in. And I think there's something exciting about being alive in uncertain times. I, for one, intend to approach the next phase of my life with the highest degree of creativity and commitment that I can muster. I know that any success I might have—and I'm defining success here in the broadest possible way—depends upon how willing I am to look ahead and take action.

Onward!

Several years ago, my mother had a chance to talk with my colleague Bob Stone, who is well into his eighties. "Bob," she said, "you must be getting ready to retire."

"No," he said. "I will never retire. Never."

And he never will. I intend to follow his example. I may not always be doing what I'm doing now. At some point, I'll probably look for a different intellectual challenge. I may try to reinvent myself in some way. But I can't imagine retiring.

In my opinion, nobody should retire. Okay, you might want to take a few months off while you're tooling up to do something new. You certainly might want to take a vacation. But retiring to play golf, perfect your bridge game, or catch up on old *New Yorkers* is giving up, and that's not a good thing.

In Chapter 1, I suggested making a list of everything you'd like to do in your life. For a young person, I wrote, putting 100 items on the list might be appropriate. For someone over fifty, it's realistic to cut that list in half. I think that's good advice. But I have to admit that even as I check off the items on my list, I keep adding more, both personal and professional. I suspect this process will never end.

One thing I know: I intend to make the next period of my life as fulfilling as possible. I assume you feel the same way. That's why I wrote this book. I hope it helps. And I hope that the next phase of your career brings you success, satisfaction, and joy.